A secret passage?

A crack of light snuck through one of the edges around the molding. Cody was sure that if he kicked it again, the door would fly open.

But before he could make another move, something started to happen. The door was opening all by itself. But it wasn't opening out, like a regular door. It was opening sideways, sliding into the wall.

Cody couldn't believe his eyes. It wasn't a door—it was a secret panel. And it wasn't opening up to the *out*side . . .

DEADTIME STORIES™
Ghost Knight

A. G. Cascone

Troll

For the real princess Gianna,
with love

and

For Roger Francis and Andrew,
the brave-hearted knights of the round table

CHAPTER 1

"Look out!" Cody Adams screamed as he braced himself for disaster.

Danger was headed his way.

Cody covered his eyes. He couldn't bear to see what was going to happen next.

"Somebody stop that maniac!"

The horrified screams coming from the corner up ahead forced Cody to take a look. He spread his fingers apart and peeked through.

Uh-oh, he thought. The danger was getting closer by the second.

Crazy old Mr. Jeevers was speeding down the street in his souped-up golf cart again. As usual, he wasn't paying any attention to where he was going.

"Lovely petunias you've got there, Mrs. Thwickle,"

Jeevers called out to the little old lady on the corner.

Mrs. Thwickle just kept screaming as she jumped out of the way of Jeevers's golf cart. Jeevers missed her by inches, but he ran right over her lovely petunias.

"Watch where you're going, you crazy old coot!" Cody's grandfather hollered at Jeevers.

Cody and his grandfather were in a golf cart too, trying their best not to get creamed by Jeevers. Cody's grandfather steered their golf cart to the far side of the road as Jeevers maneuvered his cart back onto the street.

Then Jeevers moved over too.

"Look out!" he shouted, pulling on the wheel. But he wasn't shouting at Cody and his grandfather. He was looking at something behind him. "You're lucky I didn't run right into that horse of yours," Jeevers called over his shoulder.

Horse?

Cody stood up to see whom Jeevers was talking to. But old Jeevers was only seeing things again. Meanwhile, his cart was still aimed right at Cody and his grandfather, and he wasn't looking where he was going.

"Watch out!" Cody cried, holding on for dear life.

Desperately Cody's grandfather sounded the horn.

But Jeevers didn't turn around. He just kept looking over his shoulder as his golf cart went speeding ahead.

Cody braced himself for the worst as Jeevers came right at them.

Jeevers hit them, all right. But luckily, Cody's grandfather managed to swerve just in time to avoid a head-on collision. It was just a little bump. The front fender of Jeevers's golf cart hit the back fender of their cart as Jeevers sped by.

"Jeevers!" Cody's grandfather hollered after him. "You are a menace to this community!"

"Me?" Jeevers hollered back. "What about that metal-headed, murdering madman on the horse? If I hadn't swerved out of *his* way, I would have been trampled by that monstrous beast of his. He's the menace around here," Jeevers insisted. "Why doesn't anybody ever complain about him?"

"Metal-headed, murdering madman?" Cody repeated, laughing. "Boy, Mr. Jeevers really is nuts, isn't he?" he said to his grandfather.

"Nuttier than peanut butter," Cody's grandfather answered, shaking his head. "Thank goodness he's headed away from the golf course. It's terrible trying to play when that nut burger is out on the green. He's even more dangerous on the golf course than he is on the road."

Cody's grandfather loved to play golf. He played nearly every day now that he was retired. And while Cody was visiting, his grandfather was determined to teach him how to play too.

Cody didn't have the heart to tell his grandfather he didn't really like golf. In fact, Cody thought it was every bit as boring as it looked on TV. The only cool part was driving the golf cart. Once they got on the green, Cody's grandfather always let him drive.

Driving the golf cart was one of the few fun things to

do at Shady Acres, the retirement community where Cody's grandparents lived. It was a beautiful place, located right next to the fanciest country club Cody had ever seen.

Cody's grandparents had worked hard to make his visit interesting, but after a week of being surrounded by senior citizens, Cody was ready to hang out with someone his own age.

As Cody's grandfather turned through the gates of the country club, Cody spotted Ben Cooper. Ben was the groundskeeper's son, and eleven years old, just like Cody. Cody had met Ben a few days before at the pool.

"Ben!" Cody called out as he and his grandfather headed for the clubhouse.

Ben was helping some old golfers carry their golf clubs to their cart. When he saw Cody, he smiled and waved. "What's up?"

"Not much," Cody told him. "Just playing golf with my grandfather."

"Oh." Ben sounded disappointed. "I thought maybe we could hang out together."

Cody really wanted to hang out with Ben. But he didn't want to hurt his grandfather's feelings.

Luck was on his side.

"We could really use a fourth man for our game," one of the other golfers said to Cody's grandfather. "How about it?"

Oh, please say yes, Cody pleaded silently. *Please.*

"I'd really like to help you out," Cody's grandfather

answered. "But I promised my grandson here that I'd play a round with him today."

"It's okay if you go with them, G. T.," Cody jumped in. He always called his grandfather "G. T." It was short for Grandpa Tom. "Really. I wouldn't mind at all."

"Are you sure?" G. T. asked.

"I'm positive," Cody assured him.

"I don't know." G. T. hesitated for another second. "Your grandmother will kill me if she finds out I left you alone to go play a game of golf."

Cody's grandmother had left that morning to visit her sister in the hospital. She was only going to be gone for a couple of days, but she was a nervous wreck about leaving Cody and his grandfather alone for more than ten minutes. Before she left, she'd made his grandfather promise not to let Cody out of his sight. And vice versa.

"So who's going to tell her?" Cody winked at his grandfather.

G. T. chuckled. "Okay then, mum's the word." He winked back at Cody as he climbed out of the golf cart. "Tell you what," he added. "Why don't you boys take the golf cart."

"Wow!" Cody said. "Thanks, G. T.!"

"I'll call you if I want you to come pick me up after the game," G. T. said.

"How's he going to call us if we're out driving around?" Ben asked Cody.

Cody reached into his pocket and pulled out a small cellular phone. "My grandfather got one for each of us," he told Ben. "He thought they were cooler than walkie-talkies."

"Don't forget about the shuffleboard match this afternoon," G. T. reminded Cody as he lifted his golf clubs from the cart. "I need you there to cheer my team to victory."

The grand prize for winning the shuffleboard match was season tickets to the opera. Cody's grandfather hated the opera, but his grandmother loved it. And Cody's grandfather really wanted to win so that he could hand over the opera tickets before he had to hand over her broken vase. He'd smashed it right after she'd left the house, during a pillow fight with Cody.

"I won't forget," Cody assured him, climbing into the driver's seat of the golf cart.

Ben got in on the passenger's side.

"Call me if you need me," G. T. said. "Remember, my number is 555-GOAT."

"555-GOAT?" Ben laughed. "What's your number?" he asked Cody. "555-PIG?"

"No." Cody laughed too. "Mine's just a regular number. It doesn't spell anything at all."

"Now you boys have fun," G. T. said, climbing into the cart with his friends. "And be careful. Especially if you see Jeevers coming your way."

"Don't worry," Cody called out. "We'll be careful."

"So, where should we go?" Cody asked Ben as his grandfather headed off.

"I don't know," Ben answered, thinking about it. "Have you seen the castle yet?"

"Only from the golf course," Cody said. "My grandfather said the whole building is falling down. He said it's dangerous to get too close to it."

"Yeah. That's what all the adults say," Ben shot back. "But the real reason nobody wants to get close to that castle is because it's haunted."

"No, sir." Cody laughed. He didn't believe Ben for a second. Even though he wanted to.

"Yes, sir," Ben insisted. "The whole place is crawling with ghosts. If you don't believe me, why don't we just drive over there and you can check it out yourself."

"I don't want to get in trouble," Cody told Ben.

"We won't get in any trouble," Ben assured him. "Nobody will even know we're there. Except maybe the ghosts," he added.

"Yeah, right." Cody laughed again.

"What are you, scared?" Ben prodded him.

"Hardly," Cody answered.

Ben shrugged. "Then let's go."

Cody hesitated for one more second. *Ben's dad is the groundskeeper, so Ben must know what he's talking about,* Cody decided. He hit the accelerator and drove out across the green in the direction of the castle. It was just over the hill past the eighteenth hole.

"How do you know it's haunted?" Cody asked.

"Well, first of all," Ben started, "you know that it's real, right?"

Cody nodded. "My grandfather said that some rich guy brought it over here from England, stone by stone, almost two hundred years ago."

"That's right. He was planning to live in there too," Ben told him. "But a week after he moved into the place, someone or something inside that castle chopped off his head!"

"How do you know that?" Cody asked.

"Because I heard Jeevers talking about it one day," Ben answered.

"To who?" Cody joked. "Himself?"

"As a matter of fact, yes," Ben admitted.

"Everybody knows Jeevers is nuts," Cody told Ben. "You can't believe anything he says."

"Yeah, well, my father said that the guy who lived in that castle before Shady Acres bought the property died a horrible death too," Ben added.

"Did your father say that the guy got his head chopped off?" Cody asked.

"No." Ben shook his head. "He just said the guy died a horrible death. Besides, all kinds of other terrible stuff has happened in there too."

"Like what?" Cody demanded.

"Just drive," Ben instructed. "I'll tell you when we get there."

He's just stalling so he can make up some stories, Cody thought as the golf cart climbed to the top of the hill that led to the castle. Ben was trying to make him wonder if the castle really was haunted by someone or something that chopped off people's heads.

Unfortunately, Cody wasn't going to have to wonder for long.

CHAPTER 2

"Stop here," Ben instructed Cody as the golf cart rolled out of the sun and into the eerie shadows creeping along the ground.

Cody couldn't believe his eyes as he stared at the massive stone structure looming over him. The castle looked like a haunted fortress of doom. It was bigger than any castle Cody had ever seen. Its heavy stone walls stretched the entire length of a football field. And its enormous old towers were so tall, they swallowed the sky above and blocked out the sun completely.

The castles in movies and storybooks were nowhere near as scary-looking as this one.

"Too cool," Cody said, stepping on the accelerator to get closer.

"I said, stop!" Ben shouted.

"Why?" Cody demanded as he put on the brakes. They

were about fifty feet from the castle.

"Because you don't want to park your grandfather's golf cart too close," Ben told him, sounding a little bit nervous. "You never know what kind of stuff will come flying out of those windows."

Cody followed as Ben jumped out of the cart and stepped cautiously toward the old building. "What are you talking about?" he asked.

Ben lowered his voice to a whisper. "Someone or some*thing* is always throwing stuff out of those windows up there." Ben pointed up to the top of the castle.

Cody's eyes followed Ben's finger. There were hundreds of stained glass windows in the castle. Dozens of them were smashed, as if something had been thrown through the glass.

"Once, this enormous table came flying out of there and crashed to the ground," Ben continued. "And there wasn't even any furniture in there back then."

"Get out of here." Cody knew Ben must be kidding. "If there wasn't any furniture in the place, how did a table come flying through the window?"

"I don't know," Ben said. "But it's true. And why do you think crazy old Jeevers is so crazy?"

Cody rolled his eyes. "Why?" he asked, waiting for some ridiculous answer.

"Because one day he got hit in the head with a flying brick. It came sailing right out of that window," Ben answered, pointing to one of the windows on top. "It knocked him out cold. He's been a fruitcake ever since."

There was no doubt in Cody's mind that Mr. Jeevers was a fruitcake. But Ben's explanation was harder to believe. "Did you see it happen?" he asked.

Ben hesitated. "Not in person, I didn't. But everyone knows about it."

Cody smirked. *So much for Ben's stories,* he thought. "Have you ever seen *any* of these things happen while you were here?" he asked.

"No," Ben admitted. "But I've *heard* about other stuff too."

"Like what?" Cody couldn't wait to hear what Ben would come up with next.

"After Shady Acres bought this place, they were going to try to fix up the castle and make it a fancy clubhouse," Ben told him. "But every time they tried to do any work in there, weird stuff happened."

"What kind of weird stuff?" Cody asked. "Did somebody else get his head chopped off?"

"No. But things are always disappearing in there," he told Cody. "Even people," he added dramatically.

"No way." Cody laughed.

"I'm telling you," Ben insisted. "It happened to the guy who was the groundskeeper before my father."

"The guy who used to have your father's job disappeared?" This sounded good.

"Yep," Ben said. "He went into that castle and he never came out." Ben paused. "At least not the way he was when he went in."

"So it's not like he *really* disappeared," Cody pointed out.

"Not for good," Ben explained. "But he was gone—completely gone—for two whole days. Somebody saw him go in, but nobody ever saw him come out. And for two whole days they couldn't find him anywhere. They even filed a missing persons report."

"What happened to him?" Cody asked.

"Nobody knows," Ben answered. "But one thing's for sure, whatever happened to him was pretty terrible. When they finally found the poor guy, he was hiding in the woods behind the golf course. His clothes were torn and bloody like he'd been through a battle, and he was clutching his throat. All he could say was, 'Night. Black night.' He just kept repeating that over and over, even though it was daytime when they found him."

Cody felt a chill crawl up the back of his spine. A disappearing groundskeeper was nowhere near as terrifying as someone having his head chopped off. But it was still pretty creepy.

"I'll show you the room where one of the builders saw all the blood," Ben offered.

"What blood?" Cody asked. "The groundskeeper's?"

Ben shook his head. "No. Somebody else's."

"Whose?" Cody wanted to know.

"I don't know," Ben said. "But the builder said it was all over the walls."

"Have you seen it before?" Cody asked.

"No," Ben answered. "But I know where it is."

"I thought the castle was locked up," Cody said. "That's what my grandfather told me."

16

"It is," Ben told him. "But if we climb up the front steps, we can peek through the window."

Cody could feel his heart beating against his chest as they approached the front steps of the castle. Even if Ben's stories *weren't* true, they were more than enough to send Cody's imagination into overdrive.

Especially since the castle looked even creepier up close than it did from just a short distance away. Even the air around it seemed different. As the two of them approached, Cody felt a cold breeze wrap itself around him, pulling him closer to the enormous stone stairs.

Something in Cody's head told him not to go up at all. In fact, something in Cody's head told him to turn around and run as far away from the castle as he could get. But curiosity got the better of him.

He glanced at Ben as he put his foot on the first step. "You coming?" It wasn't really a question. It was a dare.

Ben swallowed hard. Then he nodded and took the first step too.

As Cody started up the next step, a powerful gust of wind pushed him forward. Cody reached out to brace himself against the massive stone walls that lined the sides of the stairs.

Ben started to scream.

But before Cody could even turn around, he felt someone or some*thing* grab him from behind. This time it wasn't the wind pushing him forward. It was something holding him in place.

And it wasn't letting go.

"What do you two boys think you're doing here?" a deep voice growled.

Cody struggled to free himself from the hand clutching the back of his shirt. He was just about to scream for help when Ben spoke up.

"We're not doing anything, Dad," Ben answered. "We're just hanging out."

Cody heaved a sigh of relief. It was only Mr. Cooper.

"Not on the steps of this castle, you're not," Ben's father scolded.

"This is Cody Adams, Dad," Ben introduced Cody. "I met him the other day at the pool. Remember? I told you about him."

"It's nice to meet you, Cody," Mr. Cooper said, nodding at Cody. His tone changed again when he looked back at

Ben. "I told you to stay away from this castle," he barked. "So what in the world do you think you're doing here?"

"We were just, uh, checking out the stairs," Ben lied.

Ben's father grunted his disbelief. "I'll tell you what," Mr. Cooper said. "Since the two of you seem to have so much time on your hands, I've got a little job for you to do."

Now Ben grunted.

"The pool needs to be cleaned and vacuumed," his father went on.

Cody couldn't believe his bad luck. There was nothing worse than having to do chores during vacation. If he weren't trying so hard to be polite, *he* would have grunted too.

Ben's father reached into his pocket and pulled out the biggest ring of keys Cody had ever seen. He took a giant skeleton key off the ring and handed it over to Ben. "That's the key to the supply shed," he told Ben. "Go get what you need to do the job. And get to it right away."

"Sure thing, Dad," Ben said cheerfully.

Cody didn't understand why Ben suddenly seemed so happy about having to clean the pool.

"If you do a good job, I'll pay you both five dollars for it. Deal?" Ben's father said.

"Deal," Ben shot back. Then his father turned and headed away.

"This is great," Ben said, the second his father was out of earshot.

"I guess it's kind of cool that we're going to get paid,"

Cody mumbled. "But I wouldn't say it's great."

"You don't understand," Ben told him. He waved the skeleton key in front of Cody's face. "This is the key to the supply shed."

"So?" Cody shrugged. He didn't understand what was so great about that either.

"Soooo," Ben answered. "The supply shed is attached to the back of the castle. And that's where the grounds-keeper was last seen before he disappeared."

"I thought you said he went *into* the castle," Cody reminded Ben. He could practically see Ben's brain ticking away, trying to cover up his lies.

"Well, he went into the supply shed first."

Cody shot Ben a skeptical look. His stories were getting more and more unbelievable by the second.

"I'm telling you," Ben insisted. "The supply shed is just as creepy as the rest of this place. It used to be the stables—until all the horses died mysterious deaths."

Cody almost laughed in Ben's face as they reached the back of the castle. "Let's just clean the pool, okay?"

The supply shed was a low building that jutted off the main part of the castle. While Cody thought it looked like it could have been a stable, it wasn't quite as creepy as Ben wanted him to believe it was.

"You're not afraid to go inside, are you?" Ben asked.

"To see a bunch of garden tools and pool equipment?" Cody snickered. "Don't tell me you're afraid."

"*Nooooooo*," Ben answered. "But I wouldn't go in there alone," he admitted a second later. He pushed open the door and waited for Cody to step inside first.

Cody couldn't tell for sure if Ben really was afraid, or if he was just trying to scare Cody. Either way, Cody had to prove that he was brave enough to go in first.

Cody stepped through the doorway into a room that was as dark and damp as a cave. The only light came from outside, and it was easy to imagine shadowy figures lurking in the corners.

Ben came into the shed and pulled a chain. A light bulb hanging from the ceiling went on.

The bulb was bright. But the light it gave off seemed dim, as if the darkness just swallowed it up.

Cody had to admit this really *was* a creepy place.

"See. I told you," Ben said, as if he could read Cody's mind.

As Cody started looking around, the wind outside began howling up a storm. A sudden, loud *bang* made Cody's heart skip a beat. The door behind him slammed shut. Cody spun around, but he was stopped by another sound—a horrible crackling above him.

Cody looked up just as the light bulb overhead exploded with a loud pop.

Suddenly, the room was plunged into total darkness.

CHAPTER 4

"*Aaaaaaaaagh!!!*" It was pitch black in the shed. Cody couldn't even see his own hand in front of him.

His screams bounced off the walls and bumped right into Ben's.

"*Aaaaaaaaagh!!!* What happened to the light?" Ben hollered.

"The stupid bulb blew!" Cody shouted. "Open the door!"

"I can't open the door!" Ben cried back.

"What do you mean you can't open the door?" Cody's heart was pounding so hard he thought for sure it was going to pop just like the light bulb.

"I can't find it," Ben called out. "It's too dark. I can't see a thing."

"Me either," Cody said.

"Uh-oh," Ben gasped suddenly. "Maybe this is what happened to that groundskeeper before he disappeared! Maybe somebody's trying to trap us in here!"

If Ben's goal was to scare Cody, he was doing a good job. "Nobody's trying to trap us." Cody fought to stay calm. "The wind must have blown the door shut. And the stupid light bulb just blew out. That's all." At least he hoped that was all.

"Well, it must have been a tornado," Ben shot back. "Because that door weighs a ton!"

Just then, Cody felt something cold and sticky and gooey hit him in the face. He tried to jerk his head away, but the sticky, gooey thing clung to the side of his cheek!

"Ben!" Cody cried. "Something gross is trying to eat my face off!"

Ben started to scream again.

Cody had no idea what was sticking to his face. And he wasn't sure he wanted to know either—especially when he reached up to try to pull it away. It felt like a giant strip of sticky sandpaper covered with bumps . . . bumps with wings!

Cody's stomach climbed all the way up his throat. He felt like throwing up, because suddenly, he realized what was attached to his face.

A fly strip, covered with dead flies. Cody ripped the fly strip from his face so fast, it felt like he'd peeled off a layer of his own skin.

But the sting across his cheek was nowhere near as terrible as what he felt scurry across his foot.

Cody told himself that it was just a tiny field mouse—nothing to worry about. But before he could move, he felt something else creeping past him, something big and fuzzy. And whatever it was had a long, thin tail that batted against his leg.

This wasn't a tiny field mouse! It was a rat! A big, fuzzy rat!

Cody bolted forward. But he tripped over something that made a loud *clang* and fell flat on his face. Any second now the fuzzy, fat rat would start gnawing away at his flesh.

"Ben!" Cody screamed as he scrambled to his feet. "We have to get out of here! There are rats in this shed!"

When Ben heard that news, he started wailing like a siren.

"Listen to me," Cody shouted, trying not to panic. "All we have to do is get to one of the walls. Then we can feel our way around it until we find the door."

"Good idea," Ben agreed. But he refused to move until Cody came to get him.

As Cody made his way toward the sound of Ben's voice, he waved his arms in front of him, so he wouldn't run into anything else.

But it didn't help. Cody bumped into all kinds of shadowy figures anyway.

Every bang, clang, and crash sent Cody's heart racing, until he felt as though he had butterflies beating around inside his chest. No matter where Cody turned, something was waiting to strike him.

Luckily, they were things Cody recognized. Like the lawn mower. And the weed wacker.

What if there really is something worse than fly strips and rats waiting to attack in this shed? Cody thought. He forced himself to keep moving . . .

Until he bumped into something really big. Something that was alive!

"Aaaaaaagh!" Ben screamed at the top of his lungs, right in Cody's face. "Something just grabbed me!"

"It's just me!" Cody screamed back.

"Geez, oh, man," Ben huffed. "You shouldn't sneak up on people like that!"

"I wasn't sneaking up on you," Cody hollered. "I didn't even see you! Besides, you *told* me to come get you."

"Yeah," Ben shot back. *"Get* me. Not *grab* me!"

Cody wasn't about to pick a fight. "Come on," Cody said, tugging Ben's arm. "Let's just try to find the door."

After a few minutes, Cody and Ben finally made their way to one of the walls. Cody could hear voices coming from the other side of it. "You hear that?" he asked Ben.

"Yeah," Ben answered.

"The door *must* be along this wall," Cody pointed out. "I can hear people outside."

"I bet it's my dad." Ben sighed with relief. "He's probably coming to get something out of the shed."

"Hey, Dad!" Ben called through the wall. "We're stuck in here! Open the door!"

Cody ran his hand across something that felt like the molding of a door. "I think I found the door," he told Ben.

"But I can't find the knob. Maybe it fell off when the door slammed shut." Ben reached over to feel for himself.

"It feels like the door, doesn't it?" Cody asked.

"Yeah," Ben agreed. "But I can't find the knob either."

"Maybe it'll open if we just push on it," Cody said. But the door didn't budge an inch.

"Come on, you stupid door," Cody growled in frustration. Then he kicked at it as hard as he could.

A crack of light snuck through one of the edges around the molding. Cody was sure that if he kicked it again, the door would fly open.

But before he could make another move, something started to happen. The door was opening all by itself. But it wasn't opening out, like a regular door. It was opening sideways, sliding into the wall.

Cody couldn't believe his eyes. It wasn't a door—it was a secret panel. And it wasn't opening up to the *out*side.

CHAPTER

5

"What the heck is this?" Nervously, Cody peeked through the secret panel that had opened for them.

"It looks like a room," Ben answered, sounding just as scared.

"We must have found a way into the main part of the castle," Cody said. "Too cool!" Suddenly Cody felt more interested in checking out the castle than worried about bumping into ghosts.

"Where are you going?" Ben grabbed the back of Cody's shirt as Cody stepped into the room.

Cody pulled free. "Inside the castle," he told Ben. "I've never been inside a real castle before."

"Well, you're not leaving me here all alone in the dark," Ben said, following close behind.

The instant Ben said "dark," Cody realized there was

something very strange about the room they had just entered. It was full of light—only there weren't any windows.

The light was coming from above. Hundreds of candles burned in a chandelier that hung from a thirty-foot-high ceiling.

That's creepy, Cody thought as a shiver went up his spine. "I thought nobody ever came inside the castle," he said to Ben.

"Nobody does," Ben told him.

"Then who lit all these candles?" Cody asked.

"I don't know." Ben's voice cracked with fear. "And I don't want to know either! Let's just get out of here." He tugged on Cody's shirt again.

"Hang on," Cody said. "I want to look around."

"There's nothing to see," Ben said. "This isn't even the blood room."

Ben was right. The room was completely empty, except for a tapestry that hung on the far wall. Cody headed toward it to get a closer look.

"What are you doing now?" Ben asked. He was following so close behind Cody, he stepped on the back of Cody's shoe.

"Ouch," Cody hollered. He picked up his pace to get farther away from Ben. "I want to see the tapestry, okay?"

"Who cares about a stupid rug?" Ben grumbled. "And why is it hanging on the wall anyway?"

"It's not a *rug*," Cody said, rolling his eyes at Ben. "It's a tapestry. And the reason they used to hang them on the walls in castles is because big rooms like this get very cold. The stone walls are cold too. The tapestries help to keep heat in the room."

"What are you, some kind of brainiac who sits around reading encyclopedias all day?" Ben asked.

"No," Cody shot back. "I saw a show on TV about castles," he explained. "And they talked about tapestries too."

"What channel was it on?" Ben asked.

"I forget," Cody lied. He didn't want to admit to Ben that the show had been on some brainiac channel his grandparents watched. It really was a cool show—even though it *was* educational TV.

The two boys stopped in front of the enormous tapestry and stood looking at it.

"Okay," Ben said, breaking the silence. "You saw it. Now let's go."

"Wait," Cody said impatiently. "This is very interesting."

"What's so interesting about it?" Ben wasn't even looking at the tapestry. His eyes kept darting around the room as if he were waiting for something to happen.

"The guy on the show said that tapestries tell a story," Cody remembered as he studied the wall hanging.

"How can it tell a story?" Ben remarked. "There's not even any writing on it."

"It tells a story in pictures," Cody said. "Look here." He pointed to a castle in the center. "It's *this* castle," he realized. "Only in the picture, the castle's not here at Shady Acres. It's somewhere else, probably in England.

And there's a king. And a queen."

Ben nodded.

"And a beautiful princess," Cody added.

"Terrific," Ben said. "Now let's go."

Cody just ignored him as he looked up to the top left-hand corner of the tapestry, where he guessed the story began. "Wow!" he exclaimed. "It looks like there was a terrible war."

That got Ben's attention.

"Look." Cody pointed to the next picture. "The king and queen were killed. And some really scary-looking knight is holding the princess prisoner."

"Whoa," Ben said, examining the picture of the knight. "He looks like the D. C. Destroyer," he told Cody.

"The who?" Cody asked.

"The D. C. Destroyer," Ben repeated. "Don't you watch the wrestling channel?"

"Sometimes," Cody lied.

"And you don't know who the Destroyer is?"

Cody shook his head.

"He's like the biggest, baddest, meanest guy there is," Ben informed him.

"He dresses like a knight?" Cody asked.

"Nooooo," Ben hissed. "But he wears a scary black helmet just like this guy's. And he carries a big gut-ripper-outer sword too," he informed Cody. "I'm telling you," Ben went on. "If you slapped some black armor on the D.C. Destroyer, he'd look just like this guy in the tapestry."

"Well, it looks like this knight has done some destroying of his own," Cody remarked.

They both studied the next picture, which showed the castle in ruins. In front of it stood the knight in black armor, surrounded by an entire army.

Cody's eyes moved to the next picture. It was a picture of the castle again. Only it was totally rebuilt—at Shady Acres.

This is really strange, Cody thought. *This tapestry must be hundreds of years old. So how could there be a picture of the castle at Shady Acres in it?* But before he could even point that out to Ben, Ben was pointing out something else.

"Look at this!" Ben gasped. He was staring at a picture of a dark-haired man standing in front of the door to the supply shed. The man was holding a rake. In the next picture, the same man was sitting on the ground in the woods. He was clutching his throat as he lay huddled against the trunk of a tree. His clothes were all bloody and torn.

"This must be the guy who was the groundskeeper before my dad," Ben went on.

Cody's heart skipped six whole beats. Maybe Ben hadn't made up everything after all. "Who wove this tapestry?" Cody whispered.

"Not me," Ben said, looking around the room nervously again.

As Cody gazed back at the tapestry, the blood in his veins turned ice cold.

The picture of the groundskeeper was the last image in the wall hanging. But the threads used to weave the tapestry still dangled loose.

According to the TV show about castles, the dangling threads meant only one thing. The tapestry wasn't finished yet.

Someone in this castle was still working on it.

CHAPTER 6

As Cody stared at the unfinished tapestry, he began to tremble. He and Ben weren't alone. Someone or some*thing* was in the castle with them. Maybe even in the room!

Cody spun around to look. But the room was empty.

Then a loud, wailing sound echoed off the walls. Ben turned as white as a ghost. Cody was so startled, he practically hit the ceiling before he finally figured out what the sound was.

"My phone's ringing," he told Ben, reaching into his pocket. "It must be my grandfather."

But before Cody could answer the call, another sound caught his attention. At first, it was just a faint, faraway screeching. But within seconds, it had grown so loud, it completely drowned out the ringing of the phone.

"What is that?" Ben screamed, covering his ears.

"I don't know," Cody hollered back. He left the phone in his pocket and covered his ears too. But he couldn't block out the horrible noise.

It was coming from above.

When Cody looked up, he couldn't believe his eyes. Something was moving across the ceiling. Something big and black—and alive.

Cody blinked hard. *Your eyes are playing tricks on you,* he told himself. *The flickering candles from the chandelier are just casting strange shadows on the ceiling.*

He tried to convince himself that's what it was, but he couldn't—because it just wasn't true.

Ben saw it too—a huge black shadow steadily moving across the ceiling.

Within seconds, something directly above Cody dropped down. He screamed as he covered his head with his arms and jumped out of the way. But the thing never hit the ground.

When Cody looked up again, he saw why.

The thing that had dropped off the ceiling was flying around the room. It was the biggest, creepiest-looking bat Cody had ever seen. It had a wingspan as wide as an eagle's and fangs like a snake's. Its ears were furry and pointed. And it had two red eyes that glowed like fireballs.

Cody and Ben ducked as the horrid creature swooped between them.

A second bat fell from the ceiling. Then a third and a fourth.

All of a sudden it looked as though the entire ceiling was caving in.

Cody screamed out in terror as hundreds of bats took flight.

CHAPTER

7

There were so many bat wings beating at once, Cody could actually feel the draft. The breeze was blowing out the candles too.

"Let's get out of here," Cody shouted to Ben.

But Ben was frozen with fear. He didn't move. He didn't say a word. He just stood there, staring up at the ceiling, as thousands of black, fluttering wings carried hundreds of horrible, furry, fanged creatures closer and closer to the ground.

Cody grabbed Ben by his shirt and started pulling him across the room. Their only hope of escape was through the secret door.

"Hurry up," Cody hollered at Ben.

But they couldn't hurry. Because they had to dodge the swooping bats every step of the way. The hideous beasts were screeching and screaming like vicious predators as they dove straight for Cody and Ben.

Within seconds, the last two flickering candles in the chandelier blew out. As the room went dark, Cody saw the secret door sliding shut.

"Nooooo!" Cody screamed. He held on to Ben tightly as he ran for the door. With his other hand, he swatted at the bats swarming all around him. He could feel their rubbery wings slapping his flesh.

Cody knew the secret door was directly in front of him. He just hoped he could get to it before it closed completely, trapping the two of them inside the castle to be ripped to shreds by bloodthirsty bats—or something even worse!

Cody reached out in front of him, hoping to feel the secret panel. But all he felt was the hard, cold stone.

"No!" Cody screamed again. He ran his hand along the wall, frantically searching for the way out. Finally, his fingers curled around a ledge. It was the secret panel. But it was sliding shut fast.

Cody quickly squeezed through the tiny opening, pulling Ben along with him. They'd made it in the nick of time.

Click. The sound echoed off the walls behind them as the panel slid shut.

But there was no time for Cody to feel relieved. He and Ben were still in total darkness. And they were still surrounded by screaming, screeching bats. Cody could feel them clinging to his clothes and tangling themselves in his hair.

"Get me out of here!" Ben screamed. "I think one of these bats is trying to suck my blood!"

Ben swung his arms wildly, until he hit Cody in the nose.

"Ouch!" Cody said. "You broke my nose!"

"Well, you'd better hope it's not bleeding," Ben shot back. "Or one of these bats might try to bite it right off!" He kept on swinging.

"Calm down!" Cody yelled. "Or we'll never get out of here!"

Across the room, he could see a sliver of light running up the wall.

Oh, please let that be the door to the outside, Cody pleaded as he rushed toward it. He wasn't holding on to Ben anymore. He didn't have to—because Ben was clinging tightly to him.

As they got close to the light, Cody reached out, hoping to feel a doorknob this time.

"Yes!" he cried as his fingers wrapped themselves around a ball of metal.

A second later, the door flew open. Cody was practically blinded by the sun's light. But he didn't stop moving. He closed his eyes and dove through the doorway onto the ground as bats poured out overhead. Ben fell to the ground beside him.

When Cody opened his eyes, the bats were still coming out of the shed. They rose into the sky, forming a huge black cloud.

"Stay down," Cody ordered Ben.

As the two of them lay there on their stomachs with their arms covering their heads, Cody's phone rang again.

"Uh-oh," Cody murmured. "G. T.'s going to kill me for not answering this phone before." Cody reached into his pocket to get it.

"Hello," he panted.

"Cody?" his grandfather barked. "What's going on? Is something wrong?"

Plenty was wrong. Like the fact that hundreds of bats had just attacked him and Ben. But Cody couldn't possibly tell his grandfather about it. That would only get him in big, big trouble for going inside the castle in the first place.

"Uh, no, G. T.," Cody fumbled. "Nothing's wrong."

"Why didn't you answer the phone before?" G. T. asked. "I just called you a few minutes ago."

That was a good question. Cody tried to think up a good answer fast. "I left it in the golf cart while Ben and I were goofing around. I guess I didn't hear it ringing before."

"You had me worried," G. T. said, sounding a little suspicious.

"Sorry, G. T.," Cody apologized.

"Well, I just wanted to make sure you were all right," he said, "and that your phone is working."

"It's working fine, G. T.," Cody answered.

"Good," his grandfather replied. "Now hang up and call me back so I know mine is working too. Just in case you need me."

Cody couldn't believe what a worrywart his grandfather was being. "It must be working all right," Cody told him. "We're talking to each other, aren't we?"

Cody heard his grandfather chuckle on the other end of the line. "Good point," he said. "But I want to make sure my ringer's okay."

"All right," Cody sighed. He hung up the phone. Then he switched it back on and dialed 555-GOAT.

Cody listened to the ringing on the other end. When the ringing stopped, static, then a deep voice came over line.

"G. T.?" Cody said into the receiver.

The phone crackled so loudly, Cody had to yank it away from his ear. As he did, he felt a weird tingling sensation in his hand, like a tiny shock.

When Cody put the phone back to his ear, the connection was still fuzzy, but he could hear voices. Lots of screaming, scary voices, coming through the phone all at once.

"G. T.?" Cody hollered into the phone again. "Are you all right?"

Suddenly, the crackling got much louder again. Cody heard one more thing before the line went completely dead: a faraway, frightened voice pleading, *"Help me!"*

CHAPTER 8

"Ben!" Cody cried in a panic. "I think my grandfather is in some kind of trouble!"

"What kind of trouble?" Ben sounded alarmed.

"I don't know," Cody answered. "I heard someone screaming for help. And then the phone went dead."

"What do you mean, you heard someone screaming for help? Was it your grandfather or not?" Ben asked.

"I'm not sure." Cody hesitated, thinking for a second. "It sounded like a girl, but there were all kinds of weird voices screaming in the background. It was hard to tell," he admitted.

"What kind of weird voices?" Ben asked.

"Voices, voices!" Cody snapped. Couldn't Ben tell he didn't know? "Lots and lots of creepy-sounding voices!"

"Maybe you dialed the wrong number," Ben suggested.

Cody shook his head. "I'm sure I dialed it right. 555-4628. I know it by heart."

"I thought you said it was 555-GOAT," Ben shot back.

"It is!" Cody shouted. "Four, six, two, eight spells GOAT!"

"You don't have to yell," Ben told him. "Hey, maybe Jeevers hit your grandfather in the head with one of his golf balls," he said a second later. "He's always knocking people out. He swings his clubs like a million miles an hour, even when he's trying to putt."

Cody winced at the thought.

"Maybe you should just try to call him back," Ben suggested.

Cody did. But all he got was a busy signal. He held the phone out so Ben could hear it for himself.

"Maybe he's trying to call *you* back," Ben said.

Ben was right, because as soon as Cody hung up, the phone started to ring.

"Cody." G. T.'s voice came over the line. "What in the world are you doing?"

"G. T.!" Cody exclaimed. "You're okay!"

"Of course I'm okay," he said. "Why did you just hang up on me?"

"I didn't," Cody told him. "The line got real fuzzy right after you answered it. And there were all kinds of creepy voices shouting in the background. I heard somebody screaming for help just before the phone went dead. Ben thought that maybe Jeevers had hit you in the head with one of his golf balls or something."

"No, thank goodness." G. T. sounded like he was wincing at the thought this time. "The signals must have gotten crossed, that's all," he explained. "It happens sometimes with cellular phones. You must have been picking up bits and pieces of other people's conversations."

Cody was sure his grandfather was right. But he couldn't help wondering who those "other people" were, especially since one of them really was screaming for help.

"Anyway," G. T. went on, "there's nothing for you to worry about. I'm just fine. In fact, I'm heading over to the recreation center. The shuffleboard match is starting a bit early. So get over there ASAP."

"Okay, G. T.," Cody said. "We'll be there."

As Cody was about to hang up, the phone started to crackle again.

"Hello?" He pressed his ear to the receiver and listened hard. "Is somebody there?"

A second later, he got an answer.

"Help me." The frightened, faraway voice came over the line again. It was the same voice he'd heard before. It was definitely a girl.

"Who are you?" Cody shouted above the static.

The only reply he got was a loud crackle and a terrible shock. This time, it was so bad, Cody dropped the phone.

"Ouch," he cried. "That phone just zapped me!"

A strong gust of wind suddenly tore through the trees and whirled its way toward them.

It was so strong it nearly knocked Cody and Ben to the ground. As the wind wrapped itself around Cody's body, he gasped for air.

It was the creepiest thing Cody had ever felt. It was as if the wind was trying to steal his breath away and suck the life right out of him. Cody was beginning to feel light-headed and dizzy.

Finally, the burst of wind tossed him aside like a rag doll and whirled its way toward the castle, picking up twigs and dirt from the ground. As Cody fought to catch his breath, he could see the dark, forceful wind swirling up to the very top of the castle, like a tornado.

"What the heck was that?" Ben cried.

Cody didn't know. And he wasn't about to hang around to try and figure it out. He just wanted to get away from that castle, and fast. "Let's just get out of here," he told Ben as he ran for the golf cart.

"Wait," Ben called after him. "You forgot your phone!"

By now Cody didn't want to touch it. But he knew that if he left the phone behind, G. T. would be furious. So he snatched it up and jumped into the golf cart with Ben.

Cody hit the accelerator and tore away from the castle, across the golf course. But he couldn't stop himself from looking back. Something kept drawing his eyes up to the highest tower.

"Hey!" Ben punched Cody in the arm. "You're driving worse than Jeevers. Watch where you're going! You almost hit that golfer."

Cody focused his attention back on his driving.

"Sorry," he yelled to the startled lady who'd jumped out of his path.

"Where are we headed anyway?" Ben asked.

"To the recreation center," Cody told him. "I have to go watch the stupid shuffleboard match."

"Well, at least it's not near the castle," Ben said, sounding awfully relieved.

Cody nodded. He was relieved too. In fact, watching a bunch of senior citizens play shuffleboard suddenly sounded pretty good. It might be boring, but it would definitely be a *safe* way to spend the rest of the afternoon.

At least that's what Cody thought—until he heard the screams coming from the recreation center.

CHAPTER 9

"I thought you said this was supposed to be a shuffle-board match," Ben said as Cody pulled up in front of the recreation center. Loud shrieks filled the air. "It sounds more like a boxing match to me," he went on.

"I'll say," Cody agreed. "Let's find out what's going on." He hopped out of the cart and headed toward the crowd of seniors. They were gathered under the blue and white tents that shaded the shuffleboard area. G. T. stood in the center of the crowd, shaking a finger at a man with white hair and a pom-pom golf cap.

"You really are a speckle-headed cuckoo if you think we're going to forfeit this game!" G. T. shouted.

As Cody and Ben moved closer to the crowd, Cody saw whom G. T. was shouting at.

It was Mr. Jeevers. He was standing in the middle of

the commotion wearing a "Speckle-Headed Cuckoo" shirt.

"Those are the rules," Jeevers hollered back. "If you don't have a sixth Yellow-Bellied Sapsucker, your team can't play! Look it up in the rule book!"

"Jeevers is right," another Cuckoo agreed. "Mr. Goobers isn't here, so the Sapsuckers have to forfeit the game. The Speckle-Headed Cuckoos automatically win the opera tickets!"

"The Cuckoos *can't* win those opera tickets!" Cody told Ben. "My grandfather needs those tickets, or my grandmother will be really mad at him for—"

Before Cody could finish, G. T. found a sixth Yellow-Bellied Sapsucker for his team.

He grabbed Cody's shirt sleeve. "My grandson here will play for Mr. Goobers," G. T. announced proudly.

The rest of the Sapsuckers started to cheer.

"No way, G. T.!" Cody protested as his grandfather pulled him toward the playing area. "Are you crazy? I don't even know how to play shuffleboard!"

"It's easy," G. T. assured him. "Besides, you have to play or the Cuckoos will get those opera tickets."

"Why can't Mr. Goobers play?" Cody asked.

"Because Goobers went bonkers in his dance class this morning," G. T. told him. "He did some fancy dip, and now he's home with a heating pad."

Jeevers took one look at Cody and laughed. "You might as well just forfeit the game," he told G. T. "That grandson of yours is shorter than the playing sticks."

"Hey!" Ben yelled from the crowd. "Cody's going to kick all your Cuckoo butts! Aren't you, Cody?"

"That's the spirit!" G. T. cried, giving a thumbs-up.

Cody appreciated the vote of confidence. But he had a feeling that the only butt that was going to get kicked was his.

"Now let's get this match underway!" G. T. announced.

The shuffleboard looked like a giant hopscotch board, only with more blocks and much higher numbers.

Cody watched the first Cuckoo step up to the shooting line. With one quick flick of his stick, he sent the puck sliding right into the top block on the board.

The rest of the Cuckoos cheered wildly. "The score's one hundred to zero," Jeevers jeered.

Uh-oh, Cody thought. *The Cuckoos are off to a running start.*

"You might as well shoot first for the Sapsuckers," G. T. told Cody as he scooted him up to the shooting line. "That way, you can get the hang of it before the game really gets heated. Just give the puck a good shove, and aim for the block that Cuckoo just hit. It's a hundred points."

Cody wasn't about to make a fool of himself in front of a bunch of Cuckoos. But he was so nervous, his hands were starting to sweat. And he was having a really hard time trying to hold on to the stick.

"You can do it!" The Sapsuckers urged him on.

Cody took careful aim. Then he shoved the stick as hard as he could. But his hand slipped, and the puck barely slid into the first block on the board, the block with the lowest number of points.

The Cuckoos all smiled.

"That's okay," G. T. assured Cody. "You just got our team ten points. Ninety more and we'll be tied."

Cody was beginning to think Jeevers was right. The Sapsuckers should have just forfeited the game.

But by the fifth and final round, the Sapsuckers had managed to close the gap. And Cody was doing a whole lot better. On his last turn, he'd managed to score eighty points.

But the Cuckoos were still eighty points ahead with only two more shots left in the game. Jeevers's and Cody's.

"Get ready to lose, you short little whippersnapper." Jeevers chuckled as he stepped up to the line.

Jeevers lined up his shot, swinging his butt around like a hula dancer. Cody watched nervously. If Jeevers got more than twenty points, there would be no way for the Sapsuckers to win.

Cody held his breath as Jeevers finally stopped dancing and prepared to shoot.

Jeevers hit the puck so hard and so fast, it sailed right past the shuffleboard and actually took flight.

So did Jeevers's stick.

"Look out!" a little old lady screamed as the seniors standing around the court hit the deck.

Jeevers's puck soared past the crowd like a rocket, and his stick sailed straight up to the sky, tearing a hole through the top of the tent.

Cody laughed out loud as Jeevers's puck bounced off

one of the lawn statues and crashed through the club-house window.

"Way to go, Jeevers!" Ben shouted. The rest of the Sapsuckers roared with laughter.

"Interference!" Jeevers protested. "I should get to take the shot over!"

Even the rest of the Cuckoos agreed that Jeevers was nuts. Nobody was going to let him shoot again—he was way too dangerous. Besides that, Jeevers didn't have a stick anymore. It was stuck in the top of a tree.

When the commotion finally died down, Cody stepped forward to the line. The game was up to him now. If he didn't get the puck all the way up to the hundred-point block, the Cuckoos would still win the game.

"You can do it!" Ben shouted.

"Just keep your eye on your mark," G. T. advised.

Cody took a deep breath, lined up the puck, and gave it the hardest shove he could.

The crowd stood silent as the puck slid its way toward the top of the board.

For a second, Cody thought that it was going to land in the top spot. But right before it crossed the hundred-point line, it came to a stop.

"Hah!" Jeevers exclaimed triumphantly.

Cody felt his stomach sink. *There go the opera tickets,* he thought.

Then the strangest thing happened.

After coming to a complete stop, Cody's puck started moving again.

The Sapsuckers started to cheer.

Cody didn't. In fact, he felt like he was going to pass out.

Someone—or something—was pushing the puck forward!

A ghostly figure had appeared before Cody's eyes. He blinked hard, hoping that the ghost was just his imagination. But it wasn't. As the puck moved to the center of the top block, Cody saw the figure quite clearly. And it wasn't a *thing* at all.

It was a girl. A beautiful girl dressed all in pink like a storybook princess. Colorful scarves billowed from the top of her headdress and swirled around her face. But she was definitely a ghost, because Cody could see right through her!

"You did it!" G. T. cheered as the puck came to a stop right in the center of the hundred-point block. "You won the game for the Sapsuckers!"

Cody didn't say a word. He just stood there staring in amazement at the ghostly figure who'd materialized over the shuffleboard court.

"I've helped you . . . now you must help me," the ghost said, looking right at Cody. Then she dissolved into thin air.

CHAPTER 10

"No fair!" Jeevers shouted as the Sapsuckers cheered the victory. "That little pip-squeak cheated!"

"He did not," G. T. defended Cody. "He was standing behind the shooting line the whole time!"

"Yeah," Jeevers shot back. "*He* was standing there. But his little friend pushed it right in for him!"

"What little friend?" G. T. asked, laughing in Jeevers's face. "Ben?" He pointed in Ben's direction. "That boy was standing right there the whole time too!"

Cody looked at Ben. But Ben didn't look back. He just stood there, staring straight ahead—as if he'd seen a ghost too!

"Not him," Jeevers huffed. "That little girl. The one with the fancy party hat! She pushed it in!"

"What little girl with a party hat?" G. T. huffed back.

"That princess kid," Jeevers shot back.

Cody could tell by the look on G. T.'s face that G. T. thought Jeevers was insane. So did all the other seniors.

"If I were you," G. T. told Jeevers, "I wouldn't be worrying about Cody's shuffleboard puck. Because you're missing a bunch of your own marbles!"

"Yeah," another Sapsucker chimed in. "You're out of your mind, Jeevers. There was no little girl with a party hat."

"There was so!" Jeevers insisted. "She's just hard to see sometimes. She's always popping in and out of thin air. Just like that fellow on the horse."

Cody and Ben exchanged glances.

"Here we go again," G. T. groaned. "Jeevers is the only adult I know who still has imaginary friends."

"He's not my friend," Jeevers huffed. "And he's not imaginary either. I'm telling you, that fellow on the horse is the real problem around here," Jeevers continued to rant. "He thinks that just because he's in charge of that castle, he owns everything else around here too! I'm surprised that murdering madman didn't just blow in here like a big black tornado looking for that child. Because that's what he does, you know. He swirls around like a big black tornado, then blows right through you like you don't even exist!"

Cody stared at Jeevers. Maybe he wasn't as crazy as everyone thought.

"Why don't you just stop your blabbering and hand over the opera tickets," G. T. said.

"No way!" Jeevers protested. "The game was fixed!"

"It was not," the rest of the Sapsuckers chimed in.

It took a few minutes of screaming and yelling, then pushing and shoving, but finally the head Cuckoo had no choice but to give in.

"Fine," Jeevers huffed. "You Yellow Bellies can have the tickets. It doesn't matter to me. Because *I'm* going to win the golf tournament. I've been practicing every morning at the crack of dawn. I'm unbeatable."

Jeevers started to stomp away. But he had one more thing to say to Cody.

"I shall have to tell Lord Umberland about you," he snarled. "There's going to be trouble now that you're playing with that little girl. Mark my words. That metal-headed madman on the horse will not be very happy with you."

As the words left Jeevers's mouth, Cody saw a strong wind swirling out in the distance. It was swirling out from the castle—and it was big and black, just like Jeevers had described.

CHAPTER 11

Cody didn't want to stick around to find out if the big black tornado swirling out from the castle really was a metal-headed, murdering ghost on a horse. Especially since Jeevers claimed that the madman on the horse was going to be awfully angry at Cody.

Luckily, Cody didn't have to stick around. As soon as Jeevers stomped away, G. T. insisted that they all go out to celebrate the Sapsuckers' victory.

First they went for burgers. Then they went to get ice cream. When they had finished at the ice cream parlor, it was time to drop Ben off at home.

It was the longest evening of Cody's life. It wasn't easy trying to act like he was having fun when his mind was on something else. And there was no way Cody and Ben could talk about what had happened on the shuffleboard court—

not when they were surrounded by a bunch of senior Sapsuckers who'd spent the entire evening laughing about Jeevers and his "imaginary friends." But Cody and Ben both knew that Jeevers wasn't as cuckoo as they'd thought.

As soon as Cody and G. T. got home, G. T. turned on the TV. Of course he put on the brainiac channel again. This time it was a show about pyramids. Cody pretended to be interested, but his mind was racing with all the strange things that had happened. And he was dying to talk to Ben.

Luckily, G. T. dozed off in the middle of the show. Cody got up off the couch very slowly and very quietly. He tiptoed into the kitchen, where he'd left his cellular phone. Then he slid open the patio door and snuck outside. He wanted to be sure that G. T. didn't wake up and overhear his conversation with Ben.

"Hello." Ben picked up on the third ring.

"Ben," Cody said, relieved that it was Ben and not his dad who'd answered. "It's Cody. We've got to talk."

"Yeah, I know," Ben agreed. "Who was that girl?"

"Didn't you recognize her?" Cody asked.

"No," Ben answered. "I don't know any ghosts."

"It was the princess on the tapestry," Cody told him.

"No, sir," Ben gasped.

"Yes, sir," Cody shot back. "And are you ready for this?" Cody waited to drop an even bigger bomb.

"What?" Ben said.

"She was the one who was screaming for help on the phone."

"How do you know that?" Ben asked.

"Because I recognized her voice," Cody told him.

"When did you hear her voice?" Ben asked.

"Right before she disappeared," Cody told him. "Didn't you hear her?"

"No," Ben said. "I didn't hear anything."

"Oh, man," Cody shot back. "I can't believe you didn't hear it."

"Well, what did she say?" Ben asked.

"She said that now *I* had to help *her*," Cody said.

"Help her do what?" Ben shot back.

Before Cody could answer, the phone started to crackle. Ben got his answer all right. Only it wasn't from Cody.

"Help me right the wrongs of the past." Another voice cut through the static.

Cody just about dropped the phone. Ben did. Cody could hear it clatter to the ground.

"Who is this?" Cody managed to squeak the question out.

"I am the princess Gianna," the voice told him. "And now you must help me."

The princess Gianna?

This was too creepy. Cody wanted to hang up the phone. Instead, he tried to ignore the fact that he was talking to a ghost from a haunted castle on his cellular phone. "How can I possibly help you?" he asked slowly. "I'm just a regular kid. You're the one with all the magical powers."

"You *must* help me," Princess Gianna insisted, like it was some kind of royal command. "It is time to repay your debt. After all, it was I who helped you."

"But it wasn't like I asked you to," Cody shot back.

"You and your friend must come to the castle at midnight," Princess Gianna ordered, as if she hadn't heard a word Cody had said. "There will be people guarding the front steps, so you must go through the stables, just as you did earlier. Be there at the stroke of twelve. It will be safe for us to meet then."

"I don't want to meet," Cody mumbled. "Especially at midnight."

"You have no choice," Princess Gianna replied. "You and your friend are already in grave danger. Should you refuse to come, your fates will be out of my hands."

At that, the line went dead.

CHAPTER
12

It took a long time to convince Ben to go to the castle at midnight. And even though Ben finally agreed, Cody didn't trust him to show up all by himself. Cody insisted on picking Ben up at home in the golf cart.

By the time eleven o'clock rolled around, G. T. was tucked in his bed and out like a light. Cody had no problem sneaking out of the house. He only hoped he'd be alive after midnight so he could sneak back in again.

Driving around in a golf cart in the middle of the night was scary enough. But the idea of going to a haunted castle to meet a ghost at midnight was terrifying.

Cody thought about turning back as he drove down the deserted street that led to Ben's house.

But Princess Gianna's voice echoed through Cody's head. *Should you refuse . . . your fates will be out of my hands.* He had to go to the castle. He'd have to be out of his mind to ignore a threat from a ghost.

Cody hit the accelerator and sped down Shady Acres Lane. Ben's house was the last house on the corner, next to the golf course and not too far from the castle.

Ben was waiting under the streetlight at the end of his driveway when Cody arrived. There was a pile of articles sitting on the ground beside him.

"What's all that?" Cody asked as Ben started gathering them up.

"Things we might need," Ben told him.

"Like what?" Cody said.

"Like the key to the shed," Ben replied, holding it up.

"How'd you get that?" Cody asked.

"I slipped it off my father's key ring after he fell asleep," Ben explained.

"Good thinking," Cody said. "What else do we need?"

"A flashlight." Ben held it up for Cody to see. Then he put it in the back of the golf cart and picked up the next item. "A tool belt. Just in case we get stuck inside and have to break out."

Cody was impressed with Ben's clear thinking and good planning. But not for long.

"I also have my lucky rabbit's foot. And some garlic necklaces." Ben showed him two smelly necklaces made out of cloves of garlic on strings.

"What are they for?" Cody asked, wrinkling his nose.

"To protect us," Ben answered.

"Garlic only protects you from vampires," Cody shot

back. "The castle is haunted by *ghosts*."

"How do you know that?" Ben put his garlic necklace over his head. "With all those bats in there, I wouldn't be surprised if the place was loaded with vampires too. I'm not taking any chances. And if you're smart, you won't either." He held out the other garlic necklace to Cody.

"Fine." Cody took the necklace and put it on. But he didn't feel smart at all. In fact, he felt pretty stupid. "Let's go," he said.

Ben gathered up the last of his things and hopped into the golf cart.

Cody drove out over the green in the direction of the castle. This time he wasn't going so fast. He was in no real hurry to get there. He had no idea what was waiting for them. He just hoped that the princess Gianna was telling the truth when she said it would be safe.

"I can't believe you talked me into this," Ben grumbled.

"What choice do we have?" Cody replied. "If we don't go, who knows what'll happen to us. I told you what Princess Gianna said."

"Well, what's going to happen to us if we *do* go?" Ben asked.

It was the same question Cody had been asking himself. And he wasn't sure he wanted to know the answer.

"I still don't know why I have to come," Ben kept whining. "She didn't help *me* do anything."

Cody ignored him. Thankfully, Ben remained quiet until they approached the castle.

"We have to go around back," Cody said. "Princess Gianna said there would be people guarding the front steps."

"What people?" Ben yelped. "Ghost people?"

"I don't know," Cody answered, eyeing the front of the castle nervously. "I don't see anybody."

"That's because they're spooks!" Ben replied. "They're probably standing right there, waiting to kill us or something. Hurry up. Go around back, like she said."

Cody did just that. And he didn't stop until he was in front of the door to the shed. He jumped out of the cart quickly. He knew that if he hesitated for even a second, he might not be able to work up the courage to go inside.

Ben, on the other hand, stayed in his seat.

"Come on," Cody urged. "Let's go."

"I don't want to go."

"What are you, scared?" Cody taunted him.

"So what if I am?" Ben said defensively.

"Well, I am too," Cody admitted. "But we've got to do this."

Cody practically dragged Ben out of the golf cart and up to the door. "Unlock it," he told Ben.

Ben fumbled with the key until Cody finally snatched it from him and unlocked the door himself. When he looked inside the shed, the first thing he saw was that the secret panel was already open.

"Looks like someone's waiting for us," he said to Ben. Then he stepped into the shed, pulling Ben along behind him. He headed straight for the secret panel.

"Hello?" he called out as they neared the opening.

He waited for an answer. But there was none.

"Hello?" he repeated. This time he poked his head into the room.

All the candles were lit again. Only this time there were no bats. That was the first thing Cody looked for.

There were also no ghosts. Just as before, the room was empty.

The two boys stepped inside.

"What are we going to do now?" Ben asked.

"Wait, I guess," Cody answered.

"Uh-oh," Ben said, slapping his head. "We forgot all our stuff!" He turned around, about to make a run for it.

"Forget it," Cody said, grabbing the back of Ben's shirt. "We don't need it."

Cody headed over to the tapestry, dragging Ben along with him. He wanted to see if he could figure out more of the story while he waited for the princess to appear. Maybe he'd spot something that would help him understand out just what kind of ghost he was dealing with.

"Oh, no!" Cody gasped as he reached the wall hanging.

"What is it?" Ben asked, alarmed.

Cody was too stunned to speak. He just pointed at the image that had been added to the tapestry. It was a picture of him and Ben.

CHAPTER

13

"It's us!" Ben exclaimed.

Cody nodded as he continued to stare straight ahead at the startling sight. The picture woven into the tapestry *was* of the two of them—just as they were this very second—looking at the tapestry.

Every detail was so perfect, the scene almost looked like a photograph. Cody could even see the tiny little syrup stain he'd gotten on his sleeve at breakfast.

"I don't like this one bit," Ben said.

"Me neither," Cody agreed.

"What does it mean?" Ben asked.

"How should I know?" Cody snapped.

"I hope it doesn't mean that we're going to end up like that groundskeeper," Ben said.

It was exactly what Cody was thinking. He looked at

the picture of the groundskeeper cowering by the tree, his clothes bloody and torn. Then something else caught his eye.

"Look at this," he said to Ben, pointing to another section of the tapestry. It was the picture right before the one of the groundskeeper. Cody couldn't believe that he hadn't noticed it the last time.

Ben looked where Cody was pointing. "It's two guys sitting at a table having tea or something. So what?"

"Look who it is," Cody said.

Ben looked at the picture more closely, squinting to try to make out the tiny woven figures.

"It's Jeevers!" Cody finally told him.

"I don't think so," Ben disagreed.

"It is," Cody insisted. "Look. He's wearing his goofy golf cap with the pom-pom on top."

Ben looked again. "You're right," he said. "It is Jeevers. What the heck is he doing in the tapestry?"

"Beats me," Cody answered. "And who's the other guy?"

The other man in the picture looked about the same age as Jeevers. He *wasn't* dressed in golf clothes. He was dressed in medieval clothes, like the ones Cody had seen in a King Arthur movie he once watched. Still, something told Cody that the man sitting next to Jeevers was definitely *not* a movie star.

A second later Cody and Ben found out who he was.

To the boys' horror, the tapestry began to move. Frantically, Cody and Ben started backing away from it.

Cody was about to turn and run when a ghostly figure stepped out from behind the tapestry. It was the man in the royal purple robes who was having tea with Jeevers in the picture!

"Don't go," the ghostly form said to the two boys. His voice was deep and haunting, like an echo from very far away.

Ben started screaming and took off for the secret panel.

A split second later, Cody decided to follow. But it was too late. Before Cody had even taken his first step, the secret panel slammed shut.

The two boys were trapped inside the haunted chamber.

CHAPTER 14

Cody's legs felt weak as he faced the ghost.

"Welcome, brave knights." The old ghost bowed to Cody and Ben.

Brave knights? What was this guy talking about?

"We're not brave knights!" Cody told him. He didn't really have to tell him that. It was pretty obvious. Ben was screaming his head off. And Cody was so scared, his knees were still knocking together.

But the old man didn't seem to notice. Or maybe he just didn't care. Because he went right on talking as if Cody hadn't said anything at all.

"I am Lord Umberland," the ghost introduced himself. "I am the Protector of Her Royal Highness, the princess Gianna."

"Lord Umberland! You're the guy Jeevers said he was going to talk to," Cody exclaimed.

"Mr. Jeevers has a noble heart," Lord Umberland replied. "But he is somewhat befuddled, and well beyond his youth. While his company is most delightful," he went on, "he is no match for the unearthly presence that rules this castle."

What the heck is that supposed to mean? Cody wondered.

Ben was wondering the same thing. "Who the heck rules this castle?" Ben's quivering voice squeaked like a mouse.

"You will learn soon enough," Lord Umberland replied. "Come now," he told them. "Princess Gianna awaits you in the tower." He pulled the huge tapestry aside. "Take these stairs all the way to the top of the castle and you shall find her."

Jeevers wasn't the only one who was befuddled. Lord Umberland was out of his mind. There were no stairs behind the tapestry. Just a solid stone wall.

"Hurry," Lord Umberland urged them.

Neither Cody nor Ben made a move.

"There are no stairs," Cody finally pointed out.

"Of course there are," Lord Umberland insisted. "They're right here." He pointed.

Cody watched in amazement as a piece of the wall disappeared. Suddenly, a long, winding staircase stood before them.

"How did you do that?" Ben asked nervously.

"I did nothing," Lord Umberland answered.

"You just made stairs appear," Cody said.

"No." Lord Umberland smiled. "I did not. The stairs were always there. You just didn't see them until I pointed them out to you."

"How is that possible?" Cody asked.

"The more you believe, the more you will see," Lord Umberland answered. "Now you must go to my princess. There isn't much time."

"Time for what?" Cody asked as he moved slowly toward the stairs.

Lord Umberland didn't answer. All he said was "Please hurry."

Cody put his foot on the first step, testing to see if it was real. Hard stone met the bottom of his sneaker.

"Are you coming?" Cody asked, turning back to Ben.

Ben looked around the room, trying to find another way out. But there was none. "Do I have a choice?" he mumbled. Then he cautiously walked past Lord Umberland to follow Cody.

Cody glanced back to see if Lord Umberland was following them as well.

But Lord Umberland was gone. All that was left was the echo of his voice. "The stairs will take you where you need to go," he said.

Cody started climbing, with Ben close behind him.

The staircase was narrow and dimly lit. It went around in a spiral, so Cody could see only a few feet in front of him. With every step he took, he feared something terrible might be lurking just around the corner.

He was so worried about what was in front of him,

he never bothered to look behind.

Ben did.

"Uh, Cody . . ." Ben tugged on the back of Cody's shirt to get his attention. "You'd better hope there's another way down from here."

"What are you talking about?" Cody whirled around. Then he saw for himself. "Geez, oh, man," he cried. "What is going on?"

All the steps behind them had disappeared. There was nothing below but a gaping black hole.

CHAPTER 15

"What do we do now?" Ben cried.

There was only one answer. "We keep going," Cody said.

They climbed. And they climbed. And they climbed. Steps continued to appear in front of them and continued to disappear behind them. The only sound was their own footsteps echoing off the walls.

As they kept moving forward, Cody tried not to think about what was waiting for them at the top of the castle.

Suddenly a blast of cold air hit him in the face. As he rounded the next curve in the staircase, he saw the moon's light.

"We made it," he said to Ben. "We're almost at the top."

Cody bolted up the last couple of steps. The moment he reached the outside, he realized that they'd just climbed the castle's tallest tower. They were so high up,

Cody was sure he could see the whole town. What he didn't see was Princess Gianna.

"Where is she?" Ben asked as he followed Cody out onto the turret.

"I don't know," Cody answered, looking around nervously. There was no one there but the two of them.

"Good," Ben said. "She's not here. Let's go."

"Go where?" Cody asked. "There aren't any steps anymore, remember?"

"Oh, man," Ben groaned. "Now what are we going to do? That Umberland ghost is a liar. He said she'd be up here."

"Well, maybe she's coming," Cody said.

"Not up those steps, she's not," Ben said.

"Maybe she'll just pop in," Cody told him.

Ben's eyes darted back and forth. "What does she want with us anyway?" he said.

Cody wasn't paying attention to him. He was too busy looking out at the incredible view. Streetlights and house lights glowed in the darkness for miles. From where they were, he really could see all of Shady Acres.

"Look!" he told Ben. "I think I see my grandfather's house."

Ben came over to where Cody was standing. But he didn't look in the direction Cody was pointing. Instead, he leaned over the low wall and looked straight down the side of the tower.

"We're awfully high up." Ben's voice trembled. "I hate high places. They make me nervous. And I'm nervous enough as it is."

"Relax, okay?" Cody said as he started to walk across to the other side to look at the view from there. "We've got enough to worry about without you freaking out over heights."

Just then it began to get very windy. Within seconds, the wind was so strong, Cody could hear it screaming in his ears. He felt it pushing against him, pushing him back toward the low wall.

"What's going on?" Ben cried. His voice was nearly drowned out by the wailing of the wind.

"I don't know," Cody shouted back. "Maybe we should try to get back inside."

But when Cody turned toward the door, he saw that it was gone. There was no escape. They were trapped at the top of the tower with a fierce wind whipping all around them.

Cody felt himself being pushed closer and closer to the wall. The harder he fought against the wind, the harder it seemed to push him. If it didn't stop soon, Cody was afraid he would be pushed right over the edge of the tower.

There was no way in the world he'd ever survive a two-hundred-foot fall. Especially if he landed on the solid stone steps below.

"Quick!" Cody hollered at Ben. "Lie down on the ground."

But even as Cody spoke, the wind grabbed Ben from behind and lifted him off the ground.

"Noooooooo!" Ben screamed, clutching the top of the wall. But the wind was prying his fingers loose—and was about to toss him over the side.

CHAPTER

16

"Ben!" Cody cried in a panic as Ben clung to the side of the tower wall. "Hold on!"

"I can't!" Ben screamed.

"You have to!" Cody yelled as he fought to steady his own footing.

"Somebody help us!" Ben shouted while the wind whipped him repeatedly. "We're going to die!"

"We're not going to die!" Cody screamed back. "We just have to hang on!"

"To what?" Ben cried. "I can't hold on to this wall forever!"

"Grab my hand!" Cody yelled as he struggled to move toward him. He stretched out his fingers.

The wind moaned. Before Cody could grip Ben's hand, a powerful burst of air shoved him hard from behind, pushing him against the wall and almost over the edge.

"Noooooo!" Cody wailed. He struggled to keep his feet on the ground. The top half of his body was bent over the wall and he was looking straight down the side of the tower—down to certain death.

Another gust of wind inched him closer to disaster.

Cody gasped, fighting with all his might. One more gust like that and he was gone.

Then, as suddenly as it had come, the wind at his back stopped pushing and disappeared completely.

Cody panted for air. "That was a close call," he said to Ben.

"Tell me about it," Ben replied, doubling over to catch his breath too. "I thought we were dead!"

"But you're not dead." The gentle sound of another voice came from behind them.

Cody spun around.

Floating in the air was the ghostly figure he'd seen at the shuffleboard match. The same figure who was woven throughout the tapestry. It was Princess Gianna.

Cody couldn't believe his eyes. For a ghost, the princess didn't look frightening at all. She was dressed in pink, just as she had been before. And she was wearing the fancy party hat Jeevers had told everyone about. Only it wasn't really a party hat. It was a royal headdress.

As Cody stared at her face, he noticed a scar. It started on the side of her forehead and ran all the way down the side of her cheek. For a second, Cody couldn't take his eyes off it—until the moonlight caught Princess Gianna's eyes. They were deep and dark, but they glimmered like shiny cut crystal.

Cody had never seen eyes so big and so brown.

Here he was, standing face-to-face with a real ghost, and he wasn't the least bit scared.

But Ben was freaking out. "She really is a ghost!" he cried.

"Yes," Princess Gianna said. "I really am a ghost."

The moment she said the words, Cody saw tears welling up in her eyes.

"I need your help," she told them.

"Oh?" Ben shot back. "Then how come you were just trying to kill us up here?"

"I wasn't trying to kill you," Princess Gianna assured them. "It was a test to see if you were strong enough to face the Black Knight."

The Black Knight! A ripple of fear went through Cody.

"Wait a minute," he said nervously. "Are you talking about that big, black, scary-looking knight with the sharp, pointy sword? The one that killed the king and the queen in the tapestry?"

Princess Gianna nodded. "Yes," she answered sadly. "The king and the queen were my parents. And the sword the Black Knight holds is Exaltimer. He took it from my father on the field of battle. Exaltimer has magical powers," she explained. "As long as the Black Knight has the sword, he can keep us all prisoners here forever."

"So why don't you just steal that, uh, Mortimer sword back?" Ben asked.

"Exaltimer," Princess Gianna corrected him. "I've tried," she told them, pointing out the scar on the side of her cheek. "But Exaltimer must be won on the field of battle. That's why I need your help."

"What are you saying?" Cody asked. "That you want *us* to fight the Black Knight?"

"Yes," the princess answered.

"No way!" Ben shook his head. "You're not going to get me to fight a big Black Knight who has a magical gut-ripper-outer sword, and also happens to be a ghost. Something tells me that that's the way you get dead real quick!"

"You may not have a choice," Princess Gianna said. As she stared off into the distance, the look in her eyes suddenly turned to terror. "He's coming! The Black Knight is coming!"

"Where?" Ben yelped.

"Look!" Princess Gianna pointed out over the golf course toward a hill in the distance.

Cody watched in horror as a black, swirling tornado started moving toward them.

The twisting tornado whirled into a human form—the form of a metal-headed knight in black, shining armor. The sound of galloping horses thundered in the distance.

"Ben!" Cody cried. "Do you see what I see?"

Ben didn't answer. He just stood there, staring ahead with a terrified look in his eyes.

Within seconds, dozens of knights on horseback appeared, surging toward the castle. Leading them on his stallion was the knight in black armor. He held the sword, Exaltimer, over his head, swinging it wildly as if he were charging into battle.

CHAPTER 17

"You must not stay here," Princess Gianna told Cody and Ben. "Now is not the time for you to fight the Black Knight. You must fight him in a proper joust. One that is fair. One that is just."

"I don't want to fight this guy at all!" Cody insisted.

"You must go now!" the princess cried. "I will call upon you again when the time is right."

"Wait a minute!" Cody screamed as her image started to fade. "How are we supposed to get out of here? There's no stairway! And the door has disappeared!"

"You must be brave of heart and pure of spirit," Princess Gianna told them. "And remember, the more you believe, the more you will see."

With that, the princess disappeared into thin air. "There are people who will help you," her voice echoed behind her. "Believe and you will see."

"What people?" Ben cried. "We're all alone!"

Cody ran to the center of the tower where the door had been. But now it was a solid stone wall. "I believe there's a door," Cody told himself in a panic. "I believe there's a door!"

No door appeared.

"Ben!" Cody called. "It's not working! I can't make a door!"

Ben was leaning over the side of the tower, watching the knights approach. "Well, we'd better make a door," he said. "The Black Knight and his guys are almost at the castle. If they catch us up here, we're doomed."

"Please be a door," Cody begged the stone wall in front of him. "I believe you're a door!"

"Me too!" Ben said as he rushed to Cody's side. "Cross my heart and hope to die!"

Right before their eyes, the wall started to change. Suddenly a door appeared in the cold, hard stone.

"We did it!" Cody exclaimed. "We made a door!"

"Well, we'd better use it to get out of here right away," Ben said.

Cody and Ben pulled the massive stone door open as fast as they could.

"There's nothing there!" Ben cried.

Ben was right. There was nothing but blackness on the other side. Nothing but a giant, bottomless pit.

"We have to believe!" Cody told Ben. It was the only thing to do. So far it had worked. "We have to just go in and believe that the steps will be there."

Cody took a deep breath. As he stepped through the door with Ben by his side, he tried with all his might to be brave of heart.

"Oh, please let there be steps in here," Ben begged as they walked into the blackness.

Cody heaved a sigh of relief the moment he felt the solid surface beneath his feet. "Yes!" Cody exclaimed. "We made steps!"

Cody and Ben high-fived each other. But the sound of their hands clapping together was drowned out by another noise—the thunder of a thousand footsteps climbing the stairs. Cody could hear armor clanking. And then something even more terrifying

"I want their heads on a pike!" a deep voice boomed. It was the Black Knight. It had to be. "Bring me their heads on a pike!" he ordered.

Cody and Ben spun around and headed back outside, slamming the door closed behind them.

The Black Knight and his army were coming fast. And Cody had a feeling that there was no way in the world to believe them away.

CHAPTER 18

Cody didn't know what a pike was, but having his head stuck on one didn't sound like much fun!

"We're doomed," Ben moaned. "What are we going to do?"

"I don't know," Cody admitted. There was no place to run, no place to hide. And the Black Knight was only seconds away from capturing them.

A loud *clang* made Cody jump. He spun around to see what it was, sure that it meant only more trouble for them.

But he was wrong. Someone had thrown a grappling hook up over the wall.

"Quick! Climb down the rope!" a voice called out.

Cody ran to the wall and looked over the side. Two men were leaning out the window below, holding on to the other end of the rope.

Cody knew right away that they were ghosts. They were dressed in the same velvet robes that Lord Umberland wore.

"Hurry," one of the men urged him. "We'll help you escape."

"Can you climb a rope?" Cody asked Ben.

"No problem," Ben answered. "We do it in gym class all the time."

Cody quickly checked to make sure that the hook was securely attached to the wall and the rope was securely attached to the hook.

"Go," he told Ben. "And be careful."

Ben scrambled up onto the wall, got a good grip on the rope, and swung his legs over the side. Cody watched as he slid down, like a fireman on a pole. The two ghosts in the window below helped Ben inside.

"Come on," they called up to Cody.

Cody was nervous about hanging from a rope that high off the ground, but he was a lot more nervous about facing the Black Knight.

As Cody lowered himself over the wall, he saw the first of the Black Knight's men rush onto the rooftop. He slid down so fast, he got rope burns on both his hands. But he barely felt the pain. Having rope burns on his hands was a whole lot better than having his head on a pike.

Cody heaved a sigh of relief when the two ghosts eased him in through the window just as they had Ben.

"Follow us," one of the men instructed. "There's no time to waste." But he didn't go to the door. Instead, he pushed on a section of the wall. It opened to another secret passageway.

The second man hurried the two boys into the passageway behind the first man. Once they were all inside, he sealed the wall shut.

"Who are you?" Cody asked as they ran along the dark stone corridor.

The ghost in front answered. "We are Lord Umberland's sons. I am Percy, and my brother is Giles. We were sent by our father to be sure you got out of the castle safely."

"Thank goodness," Cody sighed.

"Hold your thanks," Giles told him. "You are not out yet."

They came to a stairway much like the one Cody and Ben had climbed to the top of the tower.

"Walk quietly," Percy warned as he slowed his pace.

As they moved silently down the stairs, Cody could hear voices from below. With every step they took, the voices became louder.

"Who are all those people?" Cody whispered to Percy.

"They are the lords and ladies of the castle," Percy answered.

"I told you this place was crawling with ghosts," Ben said to Cody. "I just hope we get out of here alive."

"Then you'd better be quiet," Giles said as they reached the bottom of the stairs. "There are enemies all around us."

Percy motioned for the boys to stop.

Cody didn't want to stop. The doorway to the outside was just ahead of them. All he wanted to do was run for it. But he quickly realized that would be a terrible mistake. Because between them and the doorway was the entrance to a room, and that was where the voices were coming from. The room was full of ghosts. Cody wondered if any of the Black Knight's men were in there.

Percy crept along the wall toward the entrance to the room until he was close enough to peek inside. Then he crept back toward Cody and Ben and quickly ushered them through yet another secret panel into a tiny, dark space barely bigger than a closet.

"You must stay here until the coast is clear," he whispered.

"When's that going to be?" Ben whispered back.

"Probably not until dawn," Percy answered. "Everyone in the castle is all riled up. It may be hours before the Black Knight and his men retire."

"Dawn?" Cody said a little too loudly.

"Shhh," Percy warned. "You'll be safe in here. As long as you stay silent. And as long as you stay put."

Terrific, Cody thought. Not only was there a metal-headed, murdering madman after them, *now* they had to spend the night in a haunted castle, locked in a closet with a couple of ghosts.

The hours passed slowly and silently—so slowly and silently that Cody fell asleep standing up. He didn't realize it until Giles shook him awake.

He woke Ben too.

"Come." Percy gestured as he slid open the hidden door. "It's time for you to leave."

"Move quickly," Giles instructed, pointing to the front door of the castle.

Cody *was* moving quickly, with Ben right beside him. He kept his eyes on the door, hoping with all his heart they would make it out safely. He vowed to himself that if they did, he would never, ever go anywhere near that castle again.

As they burst through the doorway, Cody saw that the sun was beginning to rise.

"We made it," he said, bounding down the steps with Ben right behind him. "And it's still early enough for me to sneak back into the house before G. T. wakes up."

"Me too," Ben said. "My parents won't be up for at least another hour."

"Yes!" Cody shouted, giving Ben the high-five.

"We're home free!" Ben cried.

Cody was sure that was true. Until another voice cut through the darkness.

"Oh, no, you're not," it said.

CHAPTER 19

"Stop right where you are!" the voice bellowed.

Cody just kept on going. But he did glance over his shoulder toward the sound of the voice.

It was Ben's dad. Cody saw him step out from behind the corner of the castle. That stopped Cody dead in his tracks.

Ben came to a stop right beside Cody. "Dad," Ben gasped, sounding more frightened of his father than of the Black Knight.

"What's going on here?" Ben's father asked, striding toward them. The expression on his face demanded a pretty good explanation.

"You're not going to believe this," Ben started.

"You boys know that nobody is allowed to go inside that castle," his father cut him off. "It's dangerous in there."

"You're telling us," Cody said without thinking.

Ben's father crossed his arms, glaring at the two of them. "You boys have a lot of explaining to do," he growled. "You can start by telling me just why you snuck out at the crack of dawn to go into that castle in the first place."

At least Ben's dad doesn't know we were out all night, Cody thought.

"We didn't really want to go in," Ben told him. "We were . . . uh, sort of tricked into it."

"Oh, really?" his father snapped.

"Really," Cody chimed in. He started to blurt out the whole story. "It all started yesterday. We were in the supply shed just looking around. Then, all of a sudden, the door slammed shut and the light blew out and we were trapped in the dark. So we tried to feel our way to the door. And we thought we had found it. But it wasn't the door to the outside, it was a secret doorway into the castle."

Ben's father shook his head in disgust.

"It's true, Dad," Ben argued.

"Then why haven't *I* ever seen this secret doorway?" Ben's father asked.

"I don't know." Ben shrugged.

"We can show it to you now," Cody said. "It'll prove that we're telling the truth."

"Good idea," Ben's dad said.

Cody and Ben led the way toward the back of the castle, walking as quickly as they could.

"Just wait until you hear all the weird stuff that goes on in there," Ben said to his father.

Ben's father held up a hand and shook his head again. He didn't want to hear. "Why don't you save your stories until *after* I've seen this secret door," he said.

They walked the rest of the way in silence.

The door to the shed was wide open. Neither Cody nor Ben had bothered to close it behind them earlier.

Ben's father went inside first. "Well?" he said, glancing around the room full of maintenance equipment. "Where is this secret doorway?"

"Right there," Ben answered, pointing across the room.

But there was no secret doorway anymore, only a solid stone wall.

CHAPTER 20

"I'm telling you, Dad," Ben tried to convince him. "The secret panel was right here."

Cody could tell by the look on Mr. Cooper's face that it wasn't working.

"I've heard enough crazy stories," Ben's father said. "I have half a mind to ground you, Ben."

Cody's heart dropped to the pit of his stomach. So did Ben's jaw.

"But, Dad," Ben pleaded. "We really are telling the truth."

Ben's father just shook his head in exasperation before the wrinkles in his forehead uncrinkled a bit. "I'll tell you what," he said. "Since the two of you are up so bright and early, why don't you get the skimmer and the vacuum and head on over to the pool. You were supposed to clean it yesterday," he reminded them. "Only guess what? Today, you're doing it for free."

"Aw, Dad," Ben moaned.

"Aw, Dad, nothing," Ben's father shot back. He grabbed the pool skimmer from its hook on the wall and handed it to Ben. "Would you rather spend the rest of the day in your room?" he threatened.

Ben didn't protest anymore. And Cody certainly wasn't about to either. As Ben's father watched them, they collected what they needed to clean the pool, put it into the golf cart, and headed on their way.

Although Cody was exhausted and not thrilled about having to clean the pool, he was very happy to be away from the castle. More than anything, Cody wished he could just forget all about it.

But Ben wasn't about to let him. "I just had a horrible thought," Ben said.

Cody was afraid to ask what it was. So he didn't.

He parked the golf cart, and the two of them unloaded the equipment to carry it up to the pool.

For a moment, it seemed as though Ben had forgotten about his terrible thought. But Cody wasn't that lucky.

"You don't think the Black Knight can come out here and kill us, do you?" Ben asked, looking pale.

Cody's eyes darted around the deserted pool area. "I don't think so," he told Ben. "At least I hope not."

"Well, why couldn't he?" Ben asked, sounding panicked. "Jeevers claims to see him all over the place!"

Cody hadn't thought about that. Ben was right. Being

away from the castle didn't mean that they were safe at all. The Black Knight and his men could come get them anyway! After all, the princess Gianna had left the castle to come to the shuffleboard match!

"So what are you saying?" Cody asked.

"For all we know, the Black Knight could be right here, right now," Ben answered. "Maybe he's standing right next to us, ready to chop our heads off!"

A sudden, shrill noise startled Cody. He jumped back so fast, he almost fell into the pool.

"What the heck is that?" Ben jumped too.

"It's just my phone," Cody answered, regaining his balance. He pulled the phone out of his pocket. But he didn't click it on.

"Aren't you going to answer it?" Ben asked.

"No way," Cody told him. "What if it's the princess Gianna asking us to come help her again?"

"What if it's your grandfather?" Ben offered another possibility.

That possibility was even worse.

With all that had been going on, Cody had forgotten all about his grandfather.

"What if it *is* him?" Cody groaned. He knew that his grandfather was going to be pretty angry. He had to answer the phone.

"Hello," Cody's voice cracked with fear as he put the receiver to his ear.

For a second, all Cody heard on the other end of the phone was breathing. Then he heard a deep voice whisper, "You have a choice. You can face me in a joust and die like men. Or you can die in your beds tonight like the little maggots that you are . . ."

Cody could feel his knees begin to shake.

"Who is it?" Ben asked.

Cody swallowed hard. "It's the Black Knight," he told Ben, covering the mouthpiece. "He says if we don't agree to fight him in a joust, he'll kill us in our sleep!"

Ben's whole body started to shake.

"What are we going to do?" Cody asked, as if there were a choice.

"Tell him we'll joust!" Ben said frantically. "I don't want to die in my sleep!"

Cody's voice trembled as he spoke into the phone again. "We'll joust," he told the Black Knight.

"Good!" The Black Knight's laughter sent shivers up Cody's spine. "Be at the castle one hour before dawn tomorrow," he instructed. "And be ready to die!"

CHAPTER 21

Cody clicked off the phone and stuck it in his pocket. "We're dead," he told Ben.

"Maybe we should run away," Ben suggested.

"And go where?" Cody asked.

"Far away from here!" Ben shot back.

For a second, Cody considered it. But then a horrifying thought entered his mind.

"What if we try to run away and he follows us?" Cody said. "No matter what we do, we're doomed! There's no way out. We're going to have to face this guy."

"Are you out of your mind?" Ben demanded. "There's no way we can joust the Black Knight!"

"Maybe we can," Cody said. "I mean, there are two of us."

"Yeah," Ben shot back. "But there's like two thousand of them!"

Cody hadn't even thought about the other knights. And he didn't want to. "You don't think we have to fight all those guys, do you?" he asked Ben.

"How should I know," Ben answered. "I never had a joust before! You should have asked *him* that before you told him we would do it!"

"You're the one who said we should joust," Cody accused Ben.

Ben rolled his eyes at Cody. "I didn't think we were really planning to show up!"

Cody's head was reeling.

Ben was right. There was no way they could show up if they had to fight all those men. But they couldn't *not* show up either. Because the Black Knight would hunt them down.

"We have to find out how this jousting stuff works," Cody told Ben.

"Oh, right," Ben huffed. "How are we going to do that?"

"Wait a minute," Cody exclaimed. "I'll bet Princess Gianna could tell us!"

"And how are we supposed to talk to her?" Ben asked. "No way I'm going back to that castle!"

Cody had an idea. "The first time I heard Princess Gianna was out on the golf course, remember? When I was trying to call G. T."

"Yeah," Ben said. "So?"

"So maybe if I try dialing 555-GOAT, I can get her on the line again," he told Ben.

Cody started to dial. And the phone started to ring.

"Cody?" A voice came over the phone.

It wasn't a friendly voice, but it was one Cody recognized immediately.

"Hi, G. T.," Cody replied nervously.

"Don't 'hi' me," G. T. said. "Where are you?"

"I'm out helping Ben clean the pool," Cody answered. "I got up real early so that I could help him," he lied. "I'm sorry I didn't leave you a note, G. T. But I didn't want to wake you up."

"Well, next time you're going to leave this house at the crack of dawn with my golf cart, you'd better wake me up," G. T. said.

For the next few minutes, Cody listened as G. T. lectured him about responsibility.

He wanted to tell G. T. about the Black Knight and the princess Gianna, and all the trouble they were in. But as angry as G. T. was, Cody didn't think he would believe the story any more than Ben's father had. So Cody just apologized for his bad behavior. And after a few more minutes, G. T. finally forgave him.

"I knew it wouldn't work," Ben said as Cody hung up. "You can't just dial up a ghost."

Suddenly Cody had an idea. It was a crazy idea. But he thought it might work. "Maybe you can," he said, studying the numbers on the phone. "Maybe if I dial GHOST instead of GOAT, I'll get one."

"Then how come you didn't get a real goat when you dialed GOAT?" Ben said.

Cody ignored Ben and started to dial.

"Besides, it's too many numbers," Ben pointed out.

Cody talked right over him. "Five, Five, Five." He said the numbers out loud as he pushed them. "G-H-O-S-T."

"This is stupid," Ben warned him.

But Cody refused to believe that. Instead, he *believed* that it would work.

Nothing happened. There was no sound on the phone at all. The line was completely dead. Still, Cody kept right on believing.

It paid off.

"It's ringing!" he told Ben excitedly.

"Oh, yeah?" Ben shot back. "Well, you'd better hope our pal the head chopper doesn't answer!"

Cody's stomach tied itself into a thousand little knots.

He was about to hang up when the ringing stopped and the phone started to crackle.

Before Cody could cut the connection, a ghostly voice came onto the line.

"I've been waiting for you to call," the ghost said.

CHAPTER 22

Cody swallowed hard as he held on to the cellular phone.

"Cody." The ghostly voice said his name.

But now Cody recognized the voice and heaved a sigh of relief. "Princess Gianna!" he exclaimed. Then he stuck his tongue out at Ben. "Ben didn't think I could get you on the phone," he said to the princess. "The Black Knight just called us and said that if we don't fight him at dawn tomorrow, he'll chop off our heads in the middle of the night."

Ben nudged Cody with his elbow. "Ask her if we can just run away!"

"Of course you can," Princess Gianna answered before Cody even repeated the question.

For a second Cody felt the weight of the world being

lifted from his shoulders. *All right!* he thought. *We don't have to fight this guy!*

Then Princess Gianna went on. "But if you do run away, he will find you. The Black Knight will not rest until he has your heads on a pike."

"So what are you saying?" Cody asked. "No matter what we do, we're gonna die?"

"No," the princess answered. "If you are brave of heart and pure of spirit, you can defeat him. You must face the Black Knight," she went on. "Look to your heart, and you will find the strength that you need."

"I don't have enough strength in my heart to fight two thousand ghost knights!" Cody told her.

"You don't have to fight the entire army," the princess replied. "Once you defeat the Black Knight, you conquer the rest of his black-hearted men. I know you can do this," she assured him.

"I have to face him all by myself?" Cody asked. "Ben doesn't have to fight?"

Ben's face lit up.

"No," Princess Gianna replied. "It will take both of you to stand up against him. And with two hearts that are brave, you have the advantage."

"What did she say?" Ben asked hopefully. "I don't have to fight?"

Cody shook his head and covered the receiver. "No. She says you do have to fight. With two brave hearts, we have the advantage."

"Helmet-head's the one with the advantage," Ben said.

"He's got that Mortimer sword! We don't even have a toothpick to fight with!"

Cody started to tell the princess just that.

But before he could finish, Princess Gianna interrupted. "You don't need any weapon greater than the ones you already have."

"The ones we have," Cody repeated. "What are they?"

"Your brave and kind hearts," she answered.

Cody wondered just how brave and kind his heart was going to be when the Black Knight plunged Exaltimer right through it.

"I must leave you now," the princess said. "I will greet you tomorrow at dawn."

The line crackled.

"No, wait!" Cody tried to stop her. But the line went dead.

As Cody turned to Ben, he could feel every bit of hope —and bravery—fading.

"We'd better start looking for some really big toothpicks," he said. "Because you and I are going to need a whole lot more than our tiny little chicken hearts when the Black Knight starts swinging Exaltimer at our heads!"

CHAPTER 23

"This isn't going to work," Ben sighed hopelessly.

It was close to an hour before dawn. Cody and Ben were out in the dark, loading the "jousting equipment" they'd gathered from the supply shed onto their "steed"— G. T.'s golf cart. This time, Cody had made sure to leave G. T. a note. And when he wrote "good-bye," he couldn't help but wonder if it was his final farewell.

Ben wasn't any more confident. "We're never going to be able to fight the Black Knight with this stuff," he moaned.

"We don't have a choice," Cody insisted, grabbing the pool hose from the pile. "This is the only stuff we've got." Cody plunked the hose onto the back of the cart. "Besides, Princess Gianna said that we don't need any weapons, remember? We just have to be brave of heart."

101

Cody tried to sound convincing. But he wasn't really feeling *brave* of anything. In fact, he was sick to his stomach and scared out of his mind.

The idea of facing a ghost knight armed with a giant, head-chopping sword was terrifying. Especially since he and Ben really were going to have to fight without any real weapons of their own.

"Oh, yeah?" Ben shot back. "Well, I wonder how brave the princess Gianna's heart would be if *she* had to try and stab the Black Knight with a pool skimmer?" he huffed as he loaded it onto the golf cart.

"We're not going to stab him with a pool skimmer," Cody reminded Ben, reaching for the volleyball poles. "We're going to stab him with these." Cody held the poles out for Ben to see. "You see? They make the ends of these things really sharp so you can push them into the ground."

"Yeah, well, we'd better be able to push them through a suit of armor," Ben shot back. "Otherwise, we're dead!"

Cody tried his best to ignore him. They had spent the previous afternoon going through the phone book looking for places to buy head-chopping swords and take head-chopping lessons. But there weren't any listings under "head-chopping." There were no listings under "jousting" either.

Cody found a number for a "pony farm," but it didn't have any horses. Just ponies—the kind you rented for birthday party rides, not for head-chopping jousts with ghost knights.

"We should have gotten the pony," Ben complained.

"G. T.'s golf cart goes faster! And at least we can both fit in it!" Cody told him for the ten thousandth time.

"I still think we're going to get creamed," Ben moaned.

Cody thought so too. But one of them had to at least *pretend* to be brave of heart.

"We're not going to get creamed," Cody lied as he shoved the volleyball poles into the backseat of the golf cart.

"You'd better hope not," Ben shot back, loading the last of their weapons: the rusted old weed wacker.

"Do we have everything?" Cody asked, looking around the front of the shed, where they had piled their arsenal before loading it onto their "mount."

"It looks like it," Ben answered.

"Then I guess we're ready." Cody climbed into the driver's seat. "We can beat this guy as long as we stick together," he said, trying to sound tough. "Just like Princess Gianna said."

But Ben just stood there, like a newly planted tree shaking in the wind.

"If you don't come, I'll have to go by myself," Cody told him.

Ben hesitated for only one more second. Then he sprinted for the golf cart and got in. "Drive," he told Cody. "Before I have a chance to change my mind."

"Now that was brave of heart," Cody said, giving Ben a high-five. "Let's go slaughter that guy." Then he put his foot on the pedal and pulled away from the shed.

The instant Cody turned onto the path that led up to the castle, a blaring noise filled the air around them.

Ben nearly fell off the golf cart. "What's that?" he cried.

Cody didn't answer. He didn't have to. Because suddenly, the castle lit up before them, and they could see quite clearly where the sound was coming from.

Standing at the highest point of the lookout tower was a ghostly figure blowing a trumpet to announce that Cody and Ben were approaching.

Ghosts started to appear everywhere, popping out of thin air and filling the steps and the castle's balconies. Even the massive front lawn filled up with hundreds of ghosts.

Cody couldn't help feeling like he was driving through a time tunnel back to medieval days, when *real* knights had *real* jousts, and *real* lords and ladies looked on. It might have been exciting, if the stands hadn't been filled with ghosts and Cody hadn't been the one who had to fight the joust.

Cody wanted to slam on the brakes, turn around, and get away as fast as he could. He didn't want to listen to a crowd of ghosts cheering away while the Black Knight chopped his head off!

"Let's get out of here!" Ben said exactly what Cody was thinking.

But it was already way too late for that.

CHAPTER

24

"Welcome, brave knights," Princess Gianna greeted Cody and Ben.

As Cody brought the golf cart to a stop in front of the platform where Princess Gianna was sitting, he didn't feel like a brave knight. His stomach was churning. His head was reeling. His knees were knocking.

"You are my champions," Princess Gianna continued. "You must wear my colors into battle."

Then she stood up and pulled two scarves from her headdress.

"For luck," she told Cody as she leaned over the railing to tie the first one around his arm. She tied the other around Ben's arm.

Then Lord Umberland stepped up beside the princess to give the boys advice. "The only way to defeat the

Black Knight is to knock off his helmet," he told them. "You must expose him for the evil spirit that he is. Only then will you be able to reclaim Exaltimer for the princess."

"How are we supposed to knock off his helmet?" Ben asked.

But before Lord Umberland could answer, the ground shook with the beat of approaching hooves.

The Black Knight rode onto the field of battle atop his ferocious black steed.

Cody's last ounce of courage all but disappeared as he watched the monster rear up on its hind legs.

"Prepare to die," the Black Knight roared.

"It is time for you to take your place on the field of battle," Lord Umberland told them. He pointed to the end of the field, opposite the Black Knight.

"The fate of my kingdom is in your hands," Princess Gianna told them.

"We won't fail you," Cody promised as he drove away. He hoped it was a promise he could keep.

"We're gonna get murdelized," Ben moaned.

"No, we're not," Cody said defiantly. "We're gonna beat that scuz ball."

"How?" Ben wailed.

"By being brave of heart and pure of spirit," Cody reminded him.

At the end of the field he turned the golf cart around. Cody was prepared to do battle.

CHAPTER 25

"Let the joust begin," Lord Umberland announced. Then he dropped a white handkerchief onto the field as a signal to start.

Before Cody even pressed down on the accelerator, the Black Knight was charging toward them.

"Hit him with the pool skimmer," Cody screamed at Ben. "Aim for his head. We've got to get that helmet off."

Cody pressed the pedal all the way to the floor. The wheels of the golf cart tore up sod as it zoomed forward.

Ben grabbed the skimmer and held it as if it were a lance. He aimed it upward so that it would hit the Black Knight right in the head.

"Get him!" Cody shouted.

The Black Knight was within striking distance.

Cody could see Ben brace himself for the hit. It looked

as though he was going to make it too.

But at the very last second, the Black Knight raised Exaltimer over his head and swung it down hard. Cody heard the blade whistle as it cut through the air. Then there was a dull clang.

The Black Knight had cut the skimmer pole right in two.

Ben screamed as he dropped the little piece left in his hand.

The Black Knight soared past them on his powerful steed. His cruel laughter echoed all around them.

Cody drove straight ahead, toward the end of the field. He wanted enough room to pick up plenty of speed for their next pass.

"Grab something else to hit him with," Cody instructed Ben.

"No way!" Ben refused. "This time I'll drive and you fight him."

"There's not enough time to switch places," Cody protested. He spun the golf cart around to face the Black Knight once again.

The Black Knight had reached the opposite end of the field. He just sat there, atop his horse, watching them. It looked as though he was waiting for them to make the first move.

"Move it," Ben said, climbing over Cody to get into the driver's seat. "I am not fighting that guy again."

Cody had no choice. He moved into the other seat. Then he quickly looked through their little arsenal to choose the next weapon. He found a good one.

"Let's go!" he told Ben as he snatched up the pole from the volleyball net.

Cody made sure he had a good grip on the pole with the pointy, spearlike thing on the end of it.

Ben peeled out.

"Make sure you get close enough for me to get a good shot at him," Cody told Ben.

But Cody didn't have to worry about getting close enough. The Black Knight was coming right for him. And he didn't seem to be the least bit worried about Cody's "spear."

As the two opponents passed on the field, the Black Knight thrust out his sword. With one, swift motion, he knocked the pole from Cody's hand and stuck his sword through the roof of the golf cart.

Cody screamed as the point of Exaltimer cut into his flesh.

CHAPTER 26

"He got me!" Cody called to Ben.

Cody's hand went to his injured shoulder. His shirt was torn so badly that the sleeve was almost completely off. Cody was afraid that the Black Knight had just about sliced his arm off too.

But there was little blood. When Cody took his hand away, he saw that the blade of Exaltimer had barely nicked his skin.

"Are you okay?" Ben asked, glancing over at Cody as he continued driving.

"I think so," Cody answered, still examining the wound on his arm.

Ben started to turn the golf cart around when he got to the end of the field.

"No!" Cody shouted at Ben. "We can't face him again. He'll kill us for sure."

"We don't have much choice," Ben pointed out. "There's no way to run away now."

At the other end of the field, the Black Knight got into position for another attack.

"But we can't win," Cody said hopelessly. "He's much stronger than we are. And that Exaltimer sword is one dangerous weapon."

"We've got to knock him off his horse," Ben said. "That's the only way we're going to be able to get his helmet off."

"How are we going to do that?" Cody asked.

"I've got a plan," Ben answered. Then he stomped down on the pedal and floored it.

The golf cart shot forward. So did the Black Knight.

"What are you doing?" Cody cried.

"I'm going to crash right into him and trip his horse," Ben told him.

"No!" Cody screamed. "That's a terrible idea, Ben! We'll get trampled to death!"

But it was too late. The Black Knight was less than ten feet away from them.

Cody braced himself for the crash.

But there was no crash.

The golf cart began to pass right through the Black Knight.

But before the cart came out the other side, something else began to happen. An ice-cold wind whipped all around them. Then the air turned black, so black that Cody couldn't see a thing.

The golf cart was lifted off the ground and began to spin around and around.

Cody screamed. He and Ben were caught inside a black tornado.

CHAPTER 27

The tornado howled as it continued to spin Cody and Ben around inside it. It seemed as though it would never end.

"Now you will die!" the Black Knight's voice boomed over the roar of the tornado.

Just as quickly as the tornado had sucked them up, it spit them out. The golf cart crashed to the ground, throwing Cody and Ben out of it. They banged into each other as they tumbled over and over on the grassy field.

Finally, Cody landed flat on his back. Desperately, he sat up and tried to catch his breath.

Looming over him on his horse was the Black Knight.

"You were a fool to think you could defeat me," the Black Knight mocked Cody. "Now you will pay for that mistake."

"Cody, look out!" Ben screamed frantically.

Cody saw what was coming next. The Black Knight had raised his sword and was prepared to strike.

Cody scrambled to his feet and began to race away. But something tripped him—the big, thick hose to the pool vacuum. It must have been thrown from the golf cart along with Cody and Ben.

Cody had one last chance at survival.

He got to his feet, snatched up the pool hose, and started swinging it around his head. He had to build up enough power to hit the Black Knight hard enough to knock him from his horse.

But he never got the chance.

"Fore!" a voice cried out from somewhere in the distance.

Then there was a loud ping.

Cody stood there dumbfounded, watching in amazement as the Black Knight toppled backward and fell off his horse.

CHAPTER 28

Cody stared in disbelief at the fallen knight. He'd never even swung the hose—how had he managed to topple the Black Knight?

"Oh, man," Ben said suddenly. "Look who's come to our rescue."

Cody looked to where Ben was pointing.

Jeevers was hurrying toward them, carrying a golf club. Cody couldn't believe it. Jeevers had knocked the Black Knight from his horse with one of his wild shots. G. T. and Ben were right about Jeevers—the old man *was* dangerous on the golf course.

Cody looked at the Black Knight, who was sprawled on the ground motionless. Not only had Jeevers knocked him off his horse, he'd knocked him out cold. Crazy old Jeevers had saved Ben's and Cody's lives.

But Jeevers didn't know that.

He looked upset as he hurried over to the crowd. "Oh, my goodness," Jeevers mumbled. "What have I done now? I'm so sorry, my good man," he apologized before he noticed who it was lying on the ground.

"He's not a good man," Cody told Jeevers. "He's the metal-headed, murdering madman you're always talking about!"

"Oh, my heavens," Jeevers gasped when he realized whom he'd hit. "It is him! Serves you right," Jeevers added, staring down at the Black Knight. "Let this be a lesson to you."

The Black Knight didn't hear him. He was still out like a light.

"You must remove his helmet," Lord Umberland urged Cody. "Do it now, my good fellow!"

"Right," Cody remembered. Once he removed the helmet, the Black Knight would be defeated once and for all.

Cody walked around the Black Knight until he was standing at his head. He leaned over, got a good hold on the helmet, and gave it one hard yank. Cody stumbled backward as the helmet came off easily in his hands.

The crowd began to cheer.

But the cheers were drowned out by another sound. The loud wail of a ferocious wind tore through the air.

Cody knew exactly what it was. He looked at the Black Knight lying on the ground. But there was nobody, or rather, no body, inside the armor.

The only thing inside the metal suit was a whirling black tornado. It was growing larger by the second, working its way out.

Cody backed away, afraid that the storm would swallow him up just as it had before. The tornado moved toward him.

Cody could feel the wind whip his face. But only for a second.

The tornado began to dissipate. Then the empty armor began to disappear as well. Within seconds, even the helmet that Cody had been holding in his hands was gone.

All that was left was the sword. *Exaltimer*.

Cody bent down to pick up the sword. It weighed a ton, and he had to use both hands to lift it.

"You have saved my kingdom," Princess Gianna declared.

"Hip, hip, hooray!" the crowd cheered.

"We couldn't have done it without Jeevers," Cody said, handing Exaltimer to Princess Gianna.

"Jeevers has always been a good friend," Lord Umberland chimed in.

"Glad to help," Jeevers said.

But Cody could tell by the look on Jeevers's face that the old guy still wasn't quite sure what was going on.

The princess was still smiling at Cody. "If you hadn't had the courage to face the Black Knight on the field of battle, I would still be his prisoner. But because of you, I am free now."

Then the princess whispered something to Lord Umberland that Cody did not hear. Lord Umberland smiled at her and nodded.

"Will the three of you please kneel before the princess?" Lord Umberland requested.

Without asking any questions, they all did as they were told. Cody knelt directly in front of Princess Gianna. She looked right at him as she lifted Exaltimer and began to speak.

"For being brave of heart and pure of spirit, I knight thee." She touched the sword to Cody's shoulder. Then she lifted it over his head to touch his other shoulder. "Arise, Sir Cody, brave knight of the realm."

Then she knighted Ben. And Mr. Jeevers too.

Suddenly, Cody noticed that there were two people standing behind the princess who hadn't been there before. Cody immediately recognized them from the tapestry. They were the princess Gianna's parents, the king and queen. The three of them together looked exactly the way they did in the tapestry.

Well, almost the way they looked in the tapestry, Cody thought.

Princess Gianna turned around and handed the sword, Exaltimer, to her father, the king. Exaltimer was in the hands of its true owner. Now the picture was just right. In fact, it was perfect.

"You have restored peace to my kingdom," the king said to Cody and Ben. "I thank you, brave knights. Your bravery here today will not go unnoticed."

Lord Umberland smiled as he rolled the tapestry out in front of them. There were no more threads dangling from the bottom. Now the threads were woven together into a picture of Cody, Ben, and Jeevers standing over the defeated Black Knight.

"Too cool!" Ben exclaimed.

"May you forever be rewarded for your kind hearts," the princess Gianna said.

"Wait!" Cody cried as the princess began to fade.

But it was too late. With her words, the ghosts began to disappear. A moment later, the castle crumbled to the ground.

"What's going on?" Ben gasped.

"Looks like they're gone for good," Jeevers said sadly. "I'm going to miss tea with Lord Umberland."

"Can you believe this?" Ben asked Cody.

But Cody didn't answer. He wasn't really paying attention. He was too busy feeling proud of himself. He really *was* brave of heart. He just hoped he wouldn't have to prove it again any time soon.

CHAPTER 29

"I'm going to miss this place," Ben said, picking up a piece of the rubble that used to be the castle. "It really was pretty cool."

"Not for Princess Gianna," Cody reminded Ben.

"I know," Ben said. "I'm glad we saved her. But it was kind of neat having a haunted castle around."

"Yeah," Cody agreed. It had been kind of neat. And it had certainly made Cody's two weeks at Shady Acres the most exciting two weeks of his life.

"This place is going to be really boring without a castle full of ghosts," Ben sighed. "And it's going to be even more boring without you," he added.

Cody felt sad too. It was his last day at Shady Acres. Summer was almost over and school was starting soon. It was time for Cody to go home.

"I'll be back," Cody told his new friend. "G. T. said I can come every weekend if I want. You can come to my house too."

"Are there any haunted castles near your house?" Ben asked.

Cody laughed. "No. But there's lots of cool stuff to do."

"Nothing will ever be cooler than this was." Ben smiled proudly.

Ben was right. Nothing would ever be as cool as exploring a haunted castle and jousting with a ghost knight.

"Sir Cody!"

Cody's heart skipped a beat as a deep voice crept out of the woods behind them. *Oh, man,* Cody thought. *It's happening again.* But to his relief, it wasn't a ghost calling him. Instead, he saw a real body follow the voice out of the woods.

"Sir Cody! Sir Ben!" Jeevers rushed toward them. "I'm so glad I found you!" he panted, out of breath.

"What's wrong?" Cody asked.

"There's a fellow back there who needs our help!" Jeevers told him.

"Back where?" Ben asked, looking around suspiciously.

"In the woods," Jeevers answered. "I ran into him while I was trying to find one of my golf balls."

"Was he a real fellow?" Cody asked. "Or a ghost fellow?"

"A *green* fellow," Jeevers replied.

Cody and Ben exchanged worried looks.

"He's a short little thing with huge feet and eyes the size of saucers," Jeevers told them. "He needs to borrow your phone."

Jeevers really is crazy, thought Cody as Jeevers went on and on about the green fellow.

"He says he's in some kind of trouble with the Purple People," Jeevers explained.

"Purple People?" Ben repeated, trying not to laugh.

Jeevers nodded. "Yes. Purple People," he insisted. "One of them had six arms and three heads." Jeevers rubbed his own head, looking confused. "Or maybe it was six heads and three arms. I'm not quite sure."

An uneasy feeling went through Cody as he watched the old man's face. He looked so serious—what if he really was telling the truth?

"Anyway," Jeevers continued, "the little green fellow says that the Purple People are stirring up some intergalactic trouble. He needs to phone home to alert the Green People."

Ben started to turn green himself.

"We'd better hurry before more Purple People start landing," Jeevers said. "They're dangerous, you know."

Cody heard something humming overhead. A huge shadow spilled across the lawn.

"Oh, heavens," Jeevers gasped. "I think we're too late."

Cody looked up. Hovering above their heads was an enormous spaceship. It looked just like the spaceships Cody had seen on TV.

"Oh, no!" Ben cried out as a beam of light shot down

from the center of the spacecraft and sucked Jeevers right up!

"Uh-oh!" Cody gasped. "I think Jeevers just got invited for tea again!"

"Let's get out of here!" Ben said.

Cody thought that was a pretty good idea.

But before either one of them had even taken the first step, Cody's phone began to ring.

Cody was pretty sure the caller wasn't G. T. . . .

Get ready for more . . .

Here's a preview of the next spine-chilling book
from A. G. Cascone.

REVENGE OF THE GOBLINS

*When Nina and Sammy find themselves lost in the woods
after dark, Nina is terrified . . . especially when a light in the
distance leads them to a strange twisted tree with a door
in its trunk. Sammy decides to investigate. He pulls open
the door and steps inside. Nina knows that she will regret
it, but she follows Sammy anyway.*

Nina couldn't believe her eyes. The inside of the tree
was as big as a house—a real house. It was ten times as
wide as its trunk!

The hollowed-out wood created a giant circular room.
One side of the room was set up like a den, with a sofa
shaped like a braided pretzel with squishy green seats.
The other side looked like an upside-down kitchen,
complete with a potbellied wood-burning stove.

In the center of it all stood a long spiral staircase that led up to nowhere. Next to that was an even longer staircase that led down into the ground, under the roots of the tree.

"Check this out!" Sammy pointed to the lopsided shelves that lined the walls. Each one was loaded with long, skinny test tubes and fat, twisted jars. A bubbling red liquid boiled away in some of the test tubes, while others were filled with smoldering crystals and colored smoke.

"It looks like a mad scientist's lab," Nina said. Several jars contained wormy, peanut-shaped blobs that looked to Nina like brains. Across from the shelves was a long, jagged-edged board lined with dozens of huge eggs wrapped in pulsating purple-blue veins.

But weirdest of all was the neon glow that filled the whole place. Golden, laserlike beams of light penetrated the interior of the tree. Nina froze as she realized they were emanating from a small, shadowy figure in the corner of the room. In his hands was a glowing gold ball.

Nina gasped so loudly, Sammy jumped.

"What?" he cried as he spun around. "What's the matter?"

Nina pointed at the creepy, monsterlike little man.

"It's just a statue." Sammy laughed when he saw the small figure. "It's like a Lava lamp," he said. "Only cooler. Check it out."

Nina didn't want to check *anything* out. But Sammy wasn't about to leave until she did. Nervously she followed him across the carpet of red moss that covered the floor.

Up close, the statue wasn't anywhere near as scary as it was from across the room. In fact, it was kind of silly-looking.

Its bubbly, squished face looked like a Halloween monster mask. Its twisted, clawed feet were twice the size of its short, stumpy legs. Its long, skinny arms were double the length of its body. And its large head was way out of proportion.

The only things that didn't look silly were the creature's teeth and its claws. The teeth were a good three inches long, and the sharp, pointed claws were even longer.

"It looks like a small goblin," Nina said as she reached out to touch its cold stone face.

Sammy didn't answer. He was too busy examining the glowing ball it held in its claws. "I wonder how this thing works," he said. "It's not plugged in or anything."

"We're in a tree," Nina pointed out. "There's no electricity!"

"Maybe there are batteries in it, or something else that makes it light up." Sammy reached out to pry the luminous orb from the goblin's stone grasp.

"Don't do that!" Nina warned him.

But it was too late. The ball was already in Sammy's hands.

Suddenly, Nina felt the cold, hard statue begin to turn warm and soften under her touch. In fact, it was getting squishy and slimy, and turning a sickly green!

Nina pulled her hand away in a panic. "Sammy, look!" she cried.

Sammy was already looking. "What's going on?" he yelped.

But the answer was obvious.

The ugly goblin with the long, sharp fangs and pointed claws was coming to life!

Collect them all!

About the Author

A. G. Cascone is the pseudonym of two authors. Between them, they have written six previous books, two horror movie screenplays, and several pop songs, including one top-ten hit.

If you want to find out more about DEADTIME STORIES or A. G. Cascone, look on the World Wide Web at:
http://www.bookwire.com/titles/deadtime/

Also, we'd love to hear from you! You can write to
A. G. Cascone
c/o Troll
100 Corporate Drive
Mahwah, NJ 07430

Or you can send e-mail directly to:
agcascone@bookwire.com